OBLIVION

Liminal Books

Liminal Books is an imprint of Between the Lines Publishing. The Liminal Books name and logo are trademarks of Between the Lines Publishing.

Between the Lines Publishing
1769 Lexington Ave N., Ste 286
Roseville, MN 55113
btwnthelines.com

Published: February 2023

Original ISBN (Paperback) 978-1-958901-29-8

Original ISBN (eBook) 978-1-958901-30-4

OBLIVION

John Shepherd

Early praise for *Oblivion*

A dive into a brilliant writer's depraved psyche, Oblivion tells the story of a man on the quest to finish a book and the distractions that threaten to derail him. He shuts himself off to the world, but can't keep the world from prying in. In the meantime, we get the most brilliant excerpts of fiction-within-fiction. Even Shepherd's stops and fits are savory. Ultimately, Oblivion is the most thought-provoking, insightful, raw, introspective piece of meta-writing I've read in a while. I kept thinking what a universal conceit this is—the novelist at constant risk of being thwarted by the world. Why hasn't it been done before? And if it has, not like this? Hats off to Shepherd for carving out this wonderful niche and nailing it.

- Sidik Fofana, author of *Stories from the Tenants Downstairs*

A funny, sometimes even moving treatise on the dangers of the mythologized life, 'Oblivion' is as reflective in language as it is in theme. Shepherd uses the Chorus, the Sirens, and the anti-hero's journey to dig at the pitfalls in cliché; and a carefully blended, elastic pair of voices – narrator's and character's – to undress the indulgent presentation of the artist and expose the perils hidden beneath.

- A.L. Kim, author of *Qwan*

Cocoons

The blinds on his apartment windows rested mostly shut, letting small flashes of light through every few spaces. It was a neat space, clean, not as dark as you might think. The perimeter was covered with cheap black shelves, the faux kind you screw together from a box. Each was filled but organized, most with books, but one with old movies – that one was a mess. Besides the off-white walls, everything in the room was black. The leather couch was black; the bookshelves were black; the kitchen appliances were stainless steel but black; the frame underneath the wood-stained coffee table was black; even the interior of the front door was, curiously, painted black.

A pile of DVD cases decorated the black TV stand across from the couch, some neatly stacked, others open and flung about madly. On the screen, the menu of a DVD flashed its thirty-second display on repeat, music fading in and out, colors darting back and forth; it offered "Play," "Scene Selection," and "Extras" for a documentary on the making of the *Indiana Jones* films. The same sliver of John Williams had echoed for hours over the same cut of Harrison Ford leaping across a cave sinkhole. The sunlight flickered through the blinds in diagonal streaks over the screen that could make an impatient man turn murderous. Stacks of legal pads and notebooks – some folded, others shredded with crossed-out ink marks – were arranged across the coffee table in a row. A near-empty bottle of Johnnie Walker Black rested near the edge of the table, ready to fall to the floor if a little too much noise passed.

His cell phone rang from beneath a couch cushion, muted by his torso on top of it. He squirmed and gave a restless stretch back and forth, then settled his head back into the corner of the couch. Instinct guided his hand to the remote, also concealed somewhere between his body and a couch pillow, and his thumb found the "Play" button. He dozed again.

"Ronnie was one of the nicest..." John Rhys-Davies bellowed of the late Ronald Lacey. "He'd been a good, working actor for most of his life and had just not got anywhere. He'd actually decided to give up acting, and he became an agent! And I think it was within about three or four months of, you know, trying to represent his fellow actors, that he got cast in 'Raiders of the Lost Ark.' Which, of course, got him started again as an actor."

If there was a life, this was it.

The phone rumbled from within the couch again. He moaned in frustration and tried to move as little as possible as he slithered his hand between the cushions and retrieved it.

2

Christopher, it read.

"What is it; what do you want?" he answered dryly.

"Ah, hello," a deep voice rang through. "I see you're - well, maybe it's an exaggeration to say 'alive'."

"Perhaps. I have yet to see evidence of that." He cleared his throat.

"Ah, yes. Quite the sad boy," Christopher said.

"A rather... sad boy."

"Yes."

They exchanged grunts and obligatory laughs.

"So, old boy, how are you?"

"That depends: What day is it?"

"Sunday," Christopher was short.

"Then I dare say I'm unwell."

"And why, pray tell, are you so unwell?"

"Well, I was going to say I was unwell regardless of the day."

There was something unimaginably grand about the quippy melodrama that infused his conversations with Christopher. None of it was without levity, but over the years, it had become a truer English.

He could hear his friend grinning through the phone. "Ha. I see. Well, that's a shame."

"What is it, do you suppose, that welcomes you so eagerly to interject right as Harrison describes the sheet of glass that they placed between him and the cobra when they shot the Well of the Souls scene?"

"A-ha!" The second vowel of Christopher's laugh was always much louder and higher pitched than the rest. "Well,

3

besides wondering if you'll ever be so inclined as to emerge from carbon freeze, I wanted to tell you about last night."

"Oh, yes, of course. Just give me a moment." He slowly rose from the corner of the couch, reached for the remote, paused the DVD as Paul Freeman showcased an uncanny French accent, and reached for the Johnnie Walker.

"Okay, so, how did it go?" He took a swig.

"Well, it was interesting. Around midnight we started playing a drinking game—"

"That's a weird coincidence," he said between sips, "I was also playing drinking games by midnight. I was alone, but—"

"Ha. Very good."

"Continue."

"Yes," Christopher pressed on. "So, somebody pulled whatever the card is for Truth or Dare."

"Oh dear."

"Oh yes."

"So, what was uncovered?" He rolled his eyes at Christopher's giddiness. Perhaps with a silent, false claim, he could convince himself that he wasn't equally in need of gossip.

"Well, after a few rounds, everything was pretty tame – but then I chose 'Truth.'"

He gasped loudly, sarcastically.

Christopher indulged him with a laugh back. "And Penny asked if I'd ever been in a threesome before. I said I had, but I was more interested in finding out about them, so I flipped it around and asked who else had."

4

"Ah, yes, *very* clever, very subtle, and of course, honorable, which is your way." He sipped.

"Yes, thank you."

"And?"

"Well, I noticed Alyssa and Penny quietly nodding their heads in the affirmative."

"Oh, *really*?"

"Oh, yes. And I noticed Cody and Si *didn't!*"

"Oh, *boy*." He didn't bother to contain an earnest squeak of ironic joy.

"Yes."

"Now that *is* interesting." Stretching his arms over his head, he cracked his shoulders and back while he yawned.

"Oh, it is," Christopher fired back in turn.

"And very unfortunate," he said.

"Oh, yes."

"For Cody and Si, I should say."

"Right, that's the one." The sounds of Christopher's fingers scrunching an aluminum bag, tearing it open at the seam, harvesting a fistful of potato chips from within – probably sour cream and onion – and chomping down on them all at once overwhelmed the phone speaker.

He sighed. "Well, as interesting as this is, I feel I have to pause for a moment: When exactly are you claiming to have had a threesome of your own?"

"Well, when Emily and I were first going out – what was that, like, four years ago?"

"You're asking me?"

Christopher laughed nervously, swallowing the bits of more chips. "Right, so about four years ago, she was kind of going through an experimental phase."

"Is that so?" He switched his own phone to speaker and held it further from his head so the chips wouldn't echo in his ear as loudly.

"It is."

"Interesting. And?" He was already exhausted.

"Well, one time, she asked to bring one of her friends into bed."

"Oh yeah?"

"Yes."

"To which you, of course, the gracious and accepting gentleman, replied, 'Why certainly, sweetheart, whatever you'd like to do is okay with me.'" He snickered.

Christopher snickered with the same rhythmic breaths. "That's right."

"And?"

"Well, yeah, so that's what happened."

"I get it, but, respectfully, why've you never told me about this?'"

Christopher muttered quickly, "Well, once things got started, after a while, it was mostly just them doing stuff, and me watching."

"Oh boy."

"What?" Christopher asked.

"Oh. Oh dear," he chided.

"What?"

"I'm afraid I can't give you credit for *that*."

6

"Why?"

"Because you didn't do anything."

"I did, though," Christopher pleaded.

"As I recall from but a moment ago, you explicitly did *nothing*."

"But I was *there*, and I was, you know, being encouraging…"

"That's not helping your case here."

"What if I…*kill* you?"

He gushed more laughter back between two sips. "Yes…you'd like to, wouldn't you?"

"I most certainly would."

Neither of them had ever quite used Ron Lacey's 'Raiders' line right, but they knew what they skated around.

Settled again, he prodded, "Yes, well, if you must, continue about the evening."

"At *any* rate, I don't believe either Cody or Si noticed. I believe this is intelligence shared only among us," Christopher said.

"Oh, now that's a delightful dash of hedonism, kept only for us."

"Yes."

"Very good. You've done well."

"I know." Christopher munched on a few more chips, then crumpled their bag and tossed it aside.

"But…how are we to hang this over their heads forever if they don't even know?" he asked.

"We'll have to get them really drunk one day and reveal it to them," Christopher said.

"But it's not our place to tell them that. That's not fair to the others."

"No, no it isn't. Well, moving on…"

They laughed hard for a while.

"Well, that's all I have for now," Christopher said. "Perhaps upon more reflection, other moments of import will strike me."

"Very well. I have to be going, for the now."

"As have I."

"Then I'll speak to you imminently."

"Yeah, yeah." Christopher disappeared.

As he did every day, he thought, a friend like Christopher was an irreconcilable partner. He tossed back a long drink and walked across the room to open the blinds. It was bright out. Cars and bodies swarmed the intersection below the apartment. He checked his phone for the time. 2:35. He had only been out for seven hours – not bad. He pushed the windows open, then brought the blinds back down. A smooth breeze refreshed him. As he turned, the notebooks and scraps of paper on the table froze in his periphery, back on the coffee table. Damn – he had to do some work.

He marched back across the room, triumphantly turned off the TV, and threw the remote onto the far end of the couch. He plopped down, grabbed the nearest notebook and a ballpoint pen without a cap, and, after scratching furiously at a clean sheet of paper for a trace of ink, started peppering out words.

Time is weird. It's very clearly a fraud.
There's no such thing as time, and no reason

8

to believe there is – it's just an explanation for age. Why, then, does everything we care about revolve around a ruse?

No, junk. Truly awful. He crossed a giant X over the lines.

He desperately needed to write, but even more desperately needed *not* to write more about Sara. All the notebooks were filled with lazy, melodramatic reflections of the last few weeks and months, and it was all junk. But it was all he could bring himself to write. He breathed out in frustration and examined the Scotch again, deciding whether the layer remaining at the bottom of the bottle was enough for one drink or two. Better used as one good drink than two forgettable drinks, he thought.

He was ready to retrieve it as a reward after deciphering a good page. Begging that his stubbornness might be defeated, he snatched up the notebook again.

Start by understanding that nothing, no part of it all, was ever your choice. It was her choice. Did you think you were being smooth or thoughtful, offering every choice of a movie, a dinner restaurant, a vacation in exchange for her time? She took that and ran. And before you knew it or could do anything about it, you were loving it. You were thrilled that she was making every choice – you thought it meant she cared about the both of you infinitely. Maybe she did– that's not important. She was making the choice because it was honest. You were making the choice to make no choices You weren't really doing that all for her; you were doing it for you. You liked thinking you were letting her choose. That was your choice, just that thought. She kept doing what she needed to, to breathe. You've been suffocating so long you forgot how to do that.

So, maybe she cared deeply about you, and the two of you together, and maybe she wanted to be with you in the end. But, think to yourself, 'what have I become?' What did you turn yourself into, trying to satisfy her? Appease her? Be what you thought she wanted? First, you forgot the version of you that she loved. Then, you forgot the version of you that you loved. Then, she forgot them both – and got the fuck out of there. And you know what else? You knew it the whole time. You let it keep happening. You let yourself become a miserable reflection. And one day, it wasn't for her anymore. You resented the paparazzi: you didn't want to answer to her anymore or to be this phony replica, but you didn't have the courage to change anything, either. So, you let her make the choice again. And now, she's long gone. And now, you're such a fucked-up piece of shit that you're

10

actually beginning to believe the whole thing
wasn't somehow your fault.

He looked over the page and couldn't decide if it had any muscle or truth.

Junk, he decided. And he tore the page from the pad, crumpled it meanly, and threw it to a basket beside the TV stand that was almost full of similar, crumpled papers. He reached for the Johnnie Walker again. Losers party harder.

Penny

Some more time had passed, maybe a few hours, when the phone rang again. Penny. He sat up and stretched, counting the rings. She usually gave up after five. As the fourth began, he sighed and answered.

"Hello?"

"Hey!"

"Hi, Pen, how are you?"

"I'm good." She paused for a while, and he could hear a TV or radio in the background. "How are you? We missed you at our little party last night."

"I know, I heard it was lots of fun. I missed you all, too." *I chose to remain several hundred miles away so that I have an easy excuse to be alone when you host these shindigs.*

"So, what's new in your life?"

Dammit. She called to interrogate under the guise of banter. It would be better if she had called for some inconveniencing favor. "Nothing special, really." He had been too terse, and she had probably noticed. *Shit*. "What're you up to?" he asked, sounding very intended.

"Oh, I'm just here in the apartment, doing some redecorating 'cause I have the day off, Simon's at work."

"How's that old horse doing? Always working too much, huh?"

"Yeah, but he likes it, he's happier when he's busy, so..." Penny trailed off.

"I guess we all are," he said.

"You're not talking to me."

He breathed. "There's nothing to tell, really. Nothing happening here. Are you excited for the wedding?"

"Ugh, you really aren't going to talk to me?"

"Nope. Wedding. Your thoughts. Go."

She laughed for him. "Well, we're excited. Simon is nervous for Alyssa; I'm nervous for Cody."

"Why nervous?"

"Well...don't you think this is a little fast?"

"No, I think it's actually sweet. They're in love. I think they should get married." *I give them two years.*

"Where's the catch?"

"What catch?"

"Well, I figured you were setting up to make some witty adjustment – or improvement – to their plans."

He chuckled in flattery. "The question is: For how long will they be in love?"

She laughed harder, "And," she held out the letter 'a,' "There it is."

"I couldn't help myself."

"So, you're nervous about it, too?"

"Less nervous, more awaiting its impending collapse under the weight of their over-anticipation."

"Heh. That's sad, though. We don't want it to not work out, it's just…"

"It's just… what?"

"Well, it's just that they've been together for only, like, fifteen months, and they're getting married in three? We've been together for five years—"

"—And you're waiting for Si to sack up."

"Are you going to say anything if I say 'yes'?"

"I'd rather he just asked you on his own, so, no," he lied.

"Then…yes."

"Why are you ashamed of that?"

"Well, you're his friend, and I feel bad for putting pressure on him," she said quietly, quickly.

"Relax, it's a good thing that you want to get married. I know Si wants to. Just hold on a bit longer."

"Thank you," she sighed. "You're very reassuring. When are you visiting? I mi— we miss you."

"Probably not until the bachelor party. I've been toiling away here, trying to find the right idea for something new."

"Oh, new book?"

"That's the hope."

"I don't know how you do that."

"Just how I'm wired, I guess." *Can this just end?*

She got jumpy. "Well, the next time you visit *after* the bachelor party, I have this friend named Chloe. I actually just met her when Simon and I went out last weekend. He mentioned you, and she seemed into—"

"Ah, Pen, please, it's okay." He let her hear his impatience.

"She's very pretty."

"Penny, really, I'm not interested in seeing anyone right n—"

"Like, *very* pretty."

"Hey, seriously. I don't care what she looks like. I really am not interested in meeting anyone right now. I'm not in the mood, and, well…"

"*That's the point*. Ugh. You're stuck in there all the time; you never see anyone, you're obviously depressed. We don't like thinking that you're feeling shitty or stuck."

"Well, thanks. Thank you. Alright? But I'm fine. And I'm sure your new friend is very nice, but I'm not interested in being set up, or seeing anybody, or thinking about anybody right now."

"Have you been drinking more?" she answered.

"Pen."

"I'm serious."

"I am, too. I'm barely drinking at all. Gave up 'cause I couldn't keep up with that boyfriend of yours."

"Very funny. But you always lie when you talk about something else instead of the question."

"I'm not drinking more," he said.

"I would understand if you were."

"Thanks?"

"We never really talked about it. Do you want to?"

"I didn't even want to talk about *this*."

"You can do whatever you want; we just want you to be happy."

"Please, stop worrying. Enjoy getting ready for the wedding. If Alyssa gets any more stressed out, she's going to skin Cody and decorate the front door with him. Worry about that, not me."

"Ha! Fine. But I'm going to keep annoying you until I know you're okay."

"You don't have to do that." *Jesus Christ.*

"Too late! Talk to you later!" The phone clicked off.

That was, somehow, a shorter call than expected.

He returned from the track he had followed: around his coffee table, in and out of the kitchen and around the outline of the living room while talking on the phone and sunk into the couch. He picked up the legal pad on top of the pile of them and rummaged around for a pen, scribbling in the margins to get the ink flowing.

> Stephen Wright has an old bit that goes, "Why is it 'a penny for your thoughts,' but you've got to 'put your two cents in?' Somebody's makin' a penny."

> Some friends make you feel this way. Some friends advertise, much more strongly than they realize, that their endeavors to help you with your problems are only secondary to some ulterior motives of their own. Some friends telegraph that they're not happy, and

that the source of it is the guy they're dating, also your friend. Some friends want to use you as a redirecting beacon of their will – to frame their ideas in your words and make suggestions on their behalf. Some friends are a little too direct in the ways they complement you. And some friends, who mean well but don't realize this transparency, just have to be told 'no.'

A favor done is a favor owed. It's not that they don't actually care – they do. It's that they find, in the avenue of their concern, a back alley where they can do more profitable business, tax-free. Their channels and yours do not converge as evenly as it appears. When they say, "I know this girl I'd like you to meet – she's just your type," it means, "I want to set you up so you owe me a favor and so that I have you on my side for other politics that may arise."

The cost of your two cents should always eclipse a penny.

"Hello?" he asked into the phone, sometime later.

"You know, there are only so many years you can live off of residuals," Christopher mocked, out of breath.

"Well, I'm going for the record."

"What've you got left?"

"Maybe twenty-thousand."

"Hmm," Christopher muttered in disbelief. "Good thing you bought the place."

"Yeah."

"So, you've got what, a year?"

"More like eighteen months, the way I live." He still sort of believed that.

"Okay, call it 15 months." Christopher was much more conservative with advice than with himself.

"Fine."

"What do you think you're going to do?"

"Finish another goddamn book." *To whom did he mean to prove himself?*

"Even if you do – and, uh, I'd like to challenge you on that before we go any further – but, even if you finish and it gets put out, who says it'll make what you need?"

"I do."

"Yes, funny, good. But, really, you have to have a better plan than that."

"I don't." He stayed slumped in the couch, getting irritated.

"Well, I'm telling you right now, you're not moving in with me."

"Hah. In writing. Got it. That's alright."

"So?"

"Listen, I don't care if I wind up on the street at this point as long as I've got a few scraps of paper to start with." He kept his petulant laughing low.

"Get serious, for a moment, huh? This is real life, boy."

"I doubt that very much. Whatever real life was supposed to be, they always made it sound friendlier than this shit."

"You have to do that for yourself. It's not just served to you."

"Ah, yes, I have to work harder. I also seem to have mislabeled my mom's phone number as 'Christopher.'"

"Haha. Really, do you not understand that you have to make something more regular happen if you're going to survive? Look, you know I think you're great. I'm not the only one. But you're not going to live like this forever. Even in the best case, eventually this life will kill you. You have to figure something else out."

"I spent years slipping into that mindset and changing my whole...let's call it my 'quest' here. You know why. You know everything – well, most everything – that I did to make it all work. Now that I'm alone again, I think I'll let myself wallow a bit longer and make this thing happen."

"You really think it'll be that good?" Christopher had put on his sullen, 'take-me-seriously' voice.

"Well, what I think doesn't matter. Look at the market. Look at how illiterate these cretins are on this ash planet. But I have a story about getting my heart smacked around that might actually interest some of them this time."

"But..."

He interrupted and method-acted some joy. "But it's really going to be good."

"Well, you have to go for it. I'm not telling you *not* to write it."

"No, just to reframe my whole thirst towards water instead of dark liquor. You just want me hydrated at the expense of a good time, eh?" he joked.

"You still miss her, eh?" Christopher bit back.

"No. It's only good business, old boy."

Rare

"I'm so glad we can do this," he said across the
table. **"It's been a while."**

"Yeah, me too." Her hair was tied in a loose bun. Her
blouse and skirt were much more conservative and grown-up
than before, but she wouldn't talk about work. He felt like a
child in his blazer and jeans. He hadn't seen her for a few
months.

"So, tell me about work. What's new?"

"Nothing really, just developing relationships with new
clients, trying to find time for my own ideas."

"Yeah, soon you'll be able to spend *all* of your time on
your own ideas."

"Let's hope so," she said quietly, then looked off to the
side.

He wondered why the exchange felt so indirect, so
unclear.

"Well, I can't wait for some perfect steak."

"Me too. I've missed it here."

"It's the best. Hopefully, we can come more often."

"Yeah…" She trailed off again.

"Folks, how are your drinks?" Their server, in a sleek black and white suit and vest, appeared from the midst of the restaurant beyond the orb of visible focus that surrounded their booth. It was too big for two people. It could probably fit six. The excess space between them and the wall made for a cold, creeping distance.

"Wonderful, thank you."

"Fantastic, thanks very much."

"Okay, great. Your dinner will be out in just a few more minutes. Can I get you anything else while you're waiting?"

They looked at each other to confirm. "No, thank you, I think we're okay," they said together.

"Okay. Be back soon."

"Remember when we did that every night?" he asked.

"I do," she said, short.

"He's good."

"Yeah, he's pretty good."

"You were better."

"I was the best." She cracked a smile and looked at him fondly.

"We're going to get everything we want and then some."

She sighed and looked away again. "Yeah…"

"Look, I'm sorry," he spit out.

"Why?"

"Come on, you know what's going on. I'm sorry I'm irritating you. I'm just trying to be reassuring."

"I don't want to do this right now." Sara was fast and certain.

"We're not doing anything. I just want to say that I understand we're not technically together right now, and I respect your space. We're both growing and getting things done, and I'm glad for that. Soon, we'll feel better about everything else, and we can be together, better than before."

"Yeah…"

It was a mistake to lay cards on the table, but he did it anyway. A silence to match the cold, open space of the booth followed.

"Here we go, folks, we have the eight-ounce fillet, medium-rare, with mashed potatoes and mixed vegetables," he placed her plate carefully on the table.

"Thank you," she said, smiling at the waiter, who did not need to know how uncomfortably the interjecting minutes had passed.

"Of course," he said, "And the New York Strip, medium-well, with a baked potato and asparagus." He placed the plate carefully on the table.

"Thank you so much," he answered, getting out the impatience he'd been holding back.

"Absolutely. Can I get you any other sides, any refills, anything at all before you get started on dinner?"

"No, I think we're doing great. Thanks again," she said.

He smiled at the server, not to be left aside in the battle to acknowledge him.

They each took a bite, smiled genuinely across the table at one another, and sighed in enjoyment. He sipped on the lip of his glass of Dewar's. She sipped on the straw of her dry martini, then stirred its pair of olives to take another.

The edge of his desk dug into the soft flesh of his forearms as he remembered the restaurant, edging closer to ten thousand words, and midnight.

> Solitude is an overrated business. There are plenty of details that create the illusion that it's consistent, independent, fun, invigorating – but it is a half-life. It's not productive, educational, or patient, and it's perilously purposeless. Even at its most challenging, any sort of partnership or teamwork has, at the least, the potential to summon something greater. The multitude of ideas, the constant argument and review, and the layers of second-guessing create detail, a more confident certainty of truth and cool. I admit, there's a difference between solitude and loneliness – the latter of which is also overrated and degenerative. But even solitude, its privileges ranging from introspective reflection to decisive ambition, has limited scope.

Before he could call himself a moron, his cell phone began to ring from across the desk. The screen, keyboard, mouse, and reference books were arranged in symmetrical rows across its face. He reached past them to find "Sara" shimmering on the screen, waiting to be answered. He stood up and slid a finger across the screen urgently.

"Hi there," he buzzed.

"Hi." The voice on the other end was tired. "How are you?"

"I'm okay, thanks, just working through some dribble to get on to a more fun chapter."

"That's good." She sounded tired.

"Thank you. How are you? What's new?"

"Nothing really," she deployed her familiar sigh, "Just wanted to see how you're doing."

"Oh, I'm doing well, thanks for asking. How are you doing?" he asked again. On autopilot, he wandered to the living room.

"I'm fine."

"That's good. Is anything new at work? Anything else interesting going on?"

She said back without waiting, "I'm sorry."

He waited a while. "What?"

"I'm sorry that I'm putting you through this."

"...It's okay. I agreed because I thought we could use more time to ourselves. It's really okay." He was already pleading.

"This is fucked up."

"No, it's not. I agreed with you, didn't I?"

"You should be with somebody else," she said.

"That's ridiculous, I don't want to be with anybody else, I want to be with you, when you're ready."

"I'm sorry."

"Please, it's okay—"

"I think we need to take this more seriously." She was breathing heavier.

"What?"

"How else can I say it?" She was nearing anger.

With a sigh, then a growl, he paced around his coffee table. He didn't know how to be kind without backing down. "Well, what do you mean by it?"

"We shouldn't see each other for a while."

"We haven't been."

"And we shouldn't talk for a while," she said with the same rhythm.

"We mostly haven't been...but...okay?"

"I'm sorry."

"It's okay." Why keep debating?

"Are you mad?" she asked.

"Well, I'm sad, but I don't understand exactly what you're saying. We're already taking a break," he pleaded again, knowing even a futile exercise keeps a few of your best muscles warm.

"Yeah."

"So, do you still want to get back together at some point?" he didn't mean to ask.

"I don't know."

"I see."

"I just don't know what I want or what to do. I need to be on my own for a while."

"I know, that's why this started." For anyone else, he'd have gotten irritated already.

"Yeah."

"Okay."

She breathed harder. "I'm really sorry, I have to go."

"Well, wait, can't we talk through this a little more? Give me a sense of what we're doing."

"I just don't know. You're going to be okay. We're going to be okay. I just need to be alone for a while," she repeated, practiced and monotone.

"Okay."

"I really have to go."

"Okay."

"Ah, shit." The phone read 'Amy Slocomb' and he sat up and cleared his throat before answering. Standing to the seven o'clock evening call, he noted it was the first time he stood up that day.

"Hello?" He began pacing between the living room and the kitchen.

"Hello."

"Amy, hi, how's it going?"

"Let's get ahead to the problem, alright?" She spoke fast and evenly, hardly downplaying an anger she couldn't be bothered to hide or to pursue. "These pages are absolute dogshit."

"I'm sorry?"

"The fifty. This is aimless, pointless dogshit. Good prose, maybe better than 'Avalon.' But nothing happens, it's clear you're not taking it anywhere. What the fuck is this?"

He didn't speak, expecting her to go on. Finally, she did.

"Well? What's the story here?"

After their first meeting, his relationship with Amy had existed entirely over the phone. A photograph on her website suggested she was in her sixties and intimidating. He had to imagine the rest: the way she probably paced around her office as he agitated her with his inconsistency; the way she must have had to bully distributors into giving obscure first-timers a chance, a mechanism to which he owed his life; the way she skated around the admission that she had grown to care about him personally – pipe dreams of validation that he'd have been the first to glean. All he really knew was that she didn't bother having a temper. She was just cold and direct enough nearly to sober him.

"Jesus, I'm sorry, Amy. Shit. I, uh… I don't know. I felt I had something strong there." He hadn't felt strongly at all; it was a gamble that she'd see, vaguely, some themes he was exploring, and then get off his ass. The gamble had missed.

"Yeah, well, what you've got are some interesting pages that hover around and don't do anything. You want to talk it out?" Spastic and unyielding, Amy mostly asked rhetorical questions.

"Yeah, alright—"

"Good. Okay. So, what're you doing with these themes? They're all over the place. You've got something interesting about age, then you abandon it. You've got something cool here with the sex stuff – then that's gone. And there's a bunch about the ex; why are you still doing that?"

He traced his fingertips over the kitchen counter delicately as he walked past it, again and again. "I guess the

28

problem is that I'm having a hard time writing about other things, but I fear it's too cliché and uninteresting to talk about romantic stuff."

Behind Amy's angry breathing, he swore he could hear the tapping of a putter on a golf ball. "Well, you're not wrong there. So, what? You're just giving me that anyway in case it's so good that we have to go through with it?"

He waited before answering. "No, I really did try other things. The things in there. But I didn't want to give you only a dozen or so pages."

She sighed and he heard her switch off the speaker and get closer to the microphone. "Look, I'm not usually interested in this romantic bullshit. I think it's played and worthless, and, frankly, after 'Avalon,' it's beneath you. But, if that's all you've got in the tank right now, go after it. Just do whatever you can, sink your teeth into it, and we'll get there."

"So, what? A post-breakup, guy-who-can't-get-his-head-out-of-his-ass thing?"

"It's the most played thing in the world, but if you get it right where you want it – give it some new ideas and some heart – we'll run with it." Amy did not want him to run with it.

"If you say so."

"No, ya little shit." She got him to chuckle. "You have to say so. One hundred by December thirtieth. With real characters, a real plot. Something we can work with. Think you can do it?"

He sighed into the phone again. It was doubtful but she was being, again, rhetorical, and he hadn't much of a choice. "Yeah, I can do it. Hey, it's me."

"Yeah, that's the problem," she said. "Alright. I still need the full draft by February."

"Yeah," he auto-piloted.

"Get it done."

"Yeah. Thanks, Amy."

Her phone clicked.

Shit.

Word Games

The most important thing about word games is whatever they're not. For he and Christopher – whose tradition of word games dated back some twelve years to their first year on a cold liberal arts campus – word games were the preferred code. They were more hieroglyph than pictogram, the details in their origins a smooth context without admission. Interrupted by dramatic social upheaval, for instance (friends breaking up with their partners or getting engaged, car accidents, deaths of tertiary high school figures, most anything), especially if it was unclear how to appropriately reply, it was customary to listen attentively to the source; then, report it to one another; then, follow with the terse and insensitive, "So, I continued pairing my socks."

And this preference only became more gratifying, perhaps alluring, upon the revelation that Salman Rushdie and Christopher Hitchens had often communicated through similar such games: presenting popular phrases highlighted by the word "heart," and replacing it with the word "dick," for example – "the dick wants what the dick wants," or, "I left my dick in San Francisco."

It was, therefore, vital that various devices of examination – an imaginary microscope, a (possibly real) stethoscope, and a real calculator – find their ways from a side table drawer to the coffee table in front of him when his cell phone rang. Buried in its usual place, the crack between two couch cushions under his back, it presented the recently edited name, "Christopher (Ignore if Between 2-4AM, Likely Related to Women)."

It was 11AM on Saturday.

"Hello, old boy. What do you want?"

"I'm afraid I've come to complain," Christopher opened.

"To complain about what?" he asked, holding court.

"Well, I had a date last night."

"Did you now?"

"I did."

"Interesting." *They were seldom interesting.*

"That I had a date? I've gotten that bad, huh?"

"No, that you're now doing with your dates what you do when you go to the casino."

"What's that?"

"You only tell me about it after, so I can't tell you not to."

They each laughed and he stretched until the lower half of his spine cracked in a delightful sequence of chimes.

"Well, you're not wrong about that, I suppose," Christopher said.

"So, if you've called to complain, I take it the date went…poorly?"

"Oh, it went poorly."

"Kindly explain. Wait, hold that thought."

He slowly rose from the couch and got his bearings, turned his phone to speaker, and shimmied across the floor to the kitchen, raising his knees as little as he could. He opened the first dark wooden cabinet on the left of the wall: empty. He searched the sink: empty.

"Where the fuck are all my glasses?"

"You don't have glasses? In your apartment?"

"I have glasses, just not the right kind."

"What kind?" Christopher mocked.

He opened the dishwasher, half-full of fresh mugs and glasses, and pulled the nearest rocks glass from its cage, skating past the row of cabinets above the kitchen counter. Across the counter, he wedged his hand through a series of dark bottles, the lights still off, the blinds letting in only a flash of sun, and pulled up a mostly empty bottle of scotch.

"Never mind, I found one," he answered.

"Alright."

He filled the glass and returned to the couch.

"So," he sat down slowly and took a sip, "as you were."

Christopher took a deep breath, playing up the drama. "Well, we had the date on the calendar for a couple of weeks—"

"Hold on, hold on; start from the beginning here. Where'd you meet this girl?"

Christopher waited as long as he could before replying, "Online—"

"Ooooh yes," he staged.

33

"What?"

"Well, you're just forcing me to wonder when, if ever, you will listen…to *me* – about anything, really, but in particular, about the need to meet women someplace besides on your phone."

"Yes, yes, I know," Christopher tried not to sound pissed.

"But?"

"Well, you know, I decided to ignore you."

"Ha. Shame. You have the confidence and the stuff of interest."

"Not sure I do, really."

"Only if you keep telling yourself that," he encouraged, not for the first time.

"Well, at any rate, we spoke for a while and finally made a date, and I was mentally preparing for it all week."

"Where'd you take her?"

"Jones and Perch."

"Jesus."

"Too much?"

"Well, yes, clearly. But I was more addressing how much it pays to work in money."

"Ah. Haha." Christopher never talked about that. "Yes, I suppose."

"Right, so, you take a girl who, poor soul, is oblivious to the Christopher *brand*, as it were, to Jones and Perch for a first date – you couldn't go, like, mini-golfing…"

"It's twenty-two degrees out, *Fool*."

"Okay, not the point, fine, but…*really*? And, by the way, so what if it's twenty-two degrees out? Mini-golf is mini-golf."

Christopher laughed. "Well, yes, I had wanted to go anyway, and I liked her a lot, so I figured, why not?"

"I can think of seventeen thousand, eight hundred and twenty-one reasons why not—"

"Ahahaha, fine, fine."

"Alright, leaving that aside: what was so disappointing?" he asked, finally investing in the tale.

"Well, she got there twenty minutes late."

"So?"

"'So?'" Christopher was incensed.

"Yeah, so what? She was probably doing her makeup or got stuck in traffic or something."

"Well, I was considering all that while I waited at the table like an idiot for twenty minutes, thinking she was going to stand me up." There was precedent, unfortunately.

"But then she got there," he filled in, "So what was the problem?"

Christopher might have been spitting under interrogation. "Well, I got so nervous while I worried about that that I was just off my game for the rest of the night."

"Weren't you the one who said that being 'on your game' is bullshit?"

"Me? No, I never said that."

"Ha! Yeah. Hmm. 'If the first impression of yourself you're submitting to a date is a sales pitch, instead of whomever you'd prefer to be, you're on borrowed time.' Wasn't that how you put it?"

Before he finished the line, Christopher challenged, "Well, not all of us fall in love like Orpheus, you *dog*."

"Haha. Fine. So?"

"Well, when she finally got there, I stood up, and, thankfully, she went for a hug right away – so I didn't have to awkwardly figure out if she'd prefer a handshake."

"Well, that's good."

"It was. Then I sat back down and forgot to get her chair for her."

"Ouch. Alright. Well, that's not so terrible – I mean, not good, but not an evening-ender." *No, even these days, you only get so many chances to be chivalrous.*

"It might as well have been. I got the impression that she thought less of me - or at least of my manners, the rest of the time."

"Are you sure?" he teased. "I mean, I would never want to accuse you of getting stuck in your own head."

Christopher laughed, despite himself. "Don't be a skank. Well, no, I guess I'm not sure. But this girl was perfect from the start. She was wearing this long, black, strapless dress, her hair and makeup were all done up perfectly, she walked in really smoothly and everyone was looking at her – and she comes over to me, smiling and confident, and I'm just wearing my suit from work and look like an idiot and act like an idiot."

"Oh, dear. Yeah, I hadn't heard of the dating app you were using, reserved for Victorian statues and Venetian blinds."

"Ha! How *dare* you…" Christopher said, not asking.

He laughed charitably. "Wait. You didn't change for the date?"

36

"I was obviously going to, but then I got out of work very late and didn't have time to go all the way home and then come back into the city."

"Well, okay, so it wasn't a spectacular start. But come on, I've lived half my life walking into rooms when the music suddenly seemed to change to Joe Jackson."

"Joe Jackson?" Christopher asked.

"*Is She Really Going Out with Him?*"

"Hahaha."

"More importantly, how was the conversation?" he went on. "And how did it end?"

"Well, it gets worse."

"Of course," he mocked again, gazing with admiration at the shape of the liquid running up the inside of the glass between his eyes.

"Ha. Well, we order some drinks – well, I order a drink. I get a Glen on the rocks."

"Good choice." He gulped down some more Dewar's straight.

"Thank you," Christopher said.

"Okay, so?"

"And she orders an unsweet iced tea."

"Hey! That's a keeper!" he said.

"Haha – maybe I should give her your number."

"Better that you didn't, I'd say."

"Yeah, won't be doing that," Christopher said.

"So, what's wrong with her iced tea?"

"Well, it was too late to un-order my drink, but I didn't want to be the only one drinking."

"Oh, yes." *Only Christopher.*

"Yeah."

"Well, that's not so bad—"

"But it gets worse..."

"Hahaha. Good."

Christopher continued without pause, "So, the server leaves, and she asks, 'How was your day?' And I say, as quickly as I can, 'Not bad, I'm lucky that I like my job, so it never feels like work.'"

He chuckled. "An abject lie."

"Yeah."

"A good start to the marriage. And then?"

"So, I say, 'How about yours?' And she says, 'It was cool, I had a lot of clients to work with, so, kind of exhausting, but not bad.'"

"What does she do?" he asked.

"She's a massage therapist."

"Oh, so, I'm starting to piece things together here."

"Whatever do you mean?" Christopher asked, the admission audible through the phone.

"Well, you talk to this girl for a couple of weeks, you never mention her to me, you take her on an expensive first date, and you think it went horribly wrong when everything you've described is more or less within standard deviation."

"Okay?"

"So, you were hoping to get a massage, and didn't."

"Hahaha! I wouldn't have minded...but, no, actually. I really enjoyed our conversations over text. Seemed like we really connected."

"Well, what the hell went wrong?"

Christopher sighed. "So, we have a nice chat the rest of the night; we've already kind of gotten to know each other's political and religious, uh, states of mind, so that's all out of the way."

"Good."

"And we have plenty in common, I told her a bit about The Smiths, who she likes a lot, but hasn't heard enough of."

"Yeah, be careful of that one," he muttered.

"Oh…Yes, I'll be careful of that one."

They had a theory about new flames who claimed to be unrelenting fans of all of your favorite music (and TV shows, films, less often books) in an effort to bond. At some point, the two of them had established that, however devious, the hope to make such a connection was well-intended and not damning. Independently, neither of them fully believed that.

"Anyway, right around the time dessert comes out—"

He interrupted, "What'd you order for dessert?"

"A chocolate layer cake."

"To share? Or each?" *This line of questioning couldn't matter less – but he might think it does, and it's funny.*

"To share," Christopher said.

"Good."

"Yes. So, right around the time dessert is served – and, mind you, I didn't think it was going very well at all, to this point – she says, 'So, are you busy after this?'"

"Oh."

"Yeah. So, I say, 'No, would you like to do something?' And she says, 'Maybe we can stay in and watch a movie?'" Christopher seemed to pause for applause.

"Oh."

"Yeah – so I invited her over and she came over, and we sat down in the living room; and I asked her what she wanted to watch. We start flipping through channels. You'll never believe what she wanted to watch."

"What?"

"*Troy*," Christopher practically gushed.

"What?"

"Yeah!"

"Two words," he proffered. "Keeper."

"Hahaha. I know. She said it's one of her favorites."

"Well, alright, so you're dealing with Helen herself here."

"Yeah. So, we leave it on, and by the time Paris and Helen are making out, so are we."

"Excellent, wow – still well within the first act. Not the turn of events I was expecting."

"Well, neither is this: after a while, I moved around a bit and started to massage her shoulders." Christopher stopped nervously. "And I tried some awful line about how it was her turn to relax."

"Christ, I hope it wasn't at all like that in particular."

"It was…"

"Jesus…Why do I talk to you?"

Christopher laughed with him. "I know. I'm awful."

Not funny! "And?"

40

"Well, she allows it, she shrugs off the line, and it's all going well. And after, like, two minutes, she throws my hands off her shoulders and stands up and says, 'Sorry, I really have to go,' and picks up her coat and walks to the door. I follow and ask what's wrong and open the door for her, and she just doesn't say anything but 'sorry' again, and she leaves."

"Wow."

"Yeah."

He considered how to speak. "Well, boy, it's not a reflection on you. Obviously, she had a lot in her head; maybe the whole situation reminded her of something or somebody else, and she was overwhelmed. Maybe she felt sick and didn't know what to do. I mean, if it was all as you described – despite that horrible line, which, somehow, she forgave you for – then I think you just have to be patient and hope she calls."

"I know. I get it. It just feels so horrible to have gotten so close to someone, and we really liked each other a lot, and then the night ends like that," Christopher whined.

"I know. As a veteran of a few unrequited massages, I think you need to be a bit more patient with someone who just gave them for eight hours."

"Yeah, it's not about that. It's just that now I'm worried I did something to set her off without knowing it, and even though I can't have known, she'll associate that with me and never want to see me again."

"You can't think that way. You just can't be sure what's going on for her, and the rest of it went so well. You've got to

41

keep your hopes up. I'm sure she'll call." *He will never hear from this woman again.*

"I'm sure she won't. I'm sure that neither she, nor any other woman I find myself seeing ever again, will ever call me back. It's just not in the cards."

That's definitely possible, yeah. "I don't want to hear any part of that."

"It's true," Christopher moped, "It's just garbage. Every time something's about to work out...this."

"I must remind you, of course, at the risk of being unsympathetic, that at worst, no terrible date of yours can go useless to me."

"Oh, I know that. Enjoy the spoils of my defeat."

"Don't worry, old boy, I won't mention anything about that. It's only directed me towards the right sensation."

"Haha. Fine," Christopher said.

"Towards the right...vibration."

"Fiiiiine."

"Towards the right...encryption."

"Alriiiiight, *dick*. Quit it."

"Haha. Alright. Well, don't worry, or try not to, anyway. It's already another day, see, you *live*."

"For now. You?" Christopher sent back.

"No."

"I see."

"It'll be alright," he offered, pitying them both.

"Stop drinking before noon."

"Hahaha. Not for a while now."

"And take some time to get out of there for a bit, will you? It's a Saturday, go out or something. Get some fresh air."

"Not even tempted."

"You may be excited to wither away in there, but nobody else is."

"Sweet of them – funny, I'm not sure where they all are."

"People are busy," Christopher said.

"Very."

"One of these weekends you should come up here, we can get hammered and go out."

"That much I would do," he said.

"We'll figure that out, then."

"We shall."

"Goodbye, old boy."

"Speak to you, eventually," he said, already setting the phone down.

"If you must."

He picked up the little black notebook beside him. A different, crumby ballpoint pen was wedged in the spine. He arched his back a bit uncomfortably over the coffee table and let some tandem of recollection and wish take him over.

> At the height of its powers a massage isn't selfless. It's a duty readily volunteered for; it's an eclipsing, rewarding sport. It's a wild trapeze, and its tightrope walker is letting the spine direct him through the whole body, taking stock of the threats of infinity luring all around underneath. There's a defiant, electric warmth owed its receiver. You've got to be

adamantly thirsting to give your energy over to them, or the warmth of your hands will tingle hollow. You've got to see a thousand-foot vertical drop below you, see all the risk clear to the floor, and keep walking. If some connection is drawn from it, it's only too easy to forget exactly how thin a string separates you from the eternal – from sliding into the conditioning that, without this other body's touch, without its electric warmth, you're nothing. It's easy to fall from the rope. Or dive.

One can imagine – and has to, it seems – a fiercely awakening exchange of that heat and touch that reminds them of how mystical, how animal it is…all the space between your brain and your heart and your stomach…the sea and the rhythm of being inside your body. And one has to imagine it, if not for some concession from the intimate, because the intimate, millennia ago, absconded with the independently sensuous and sensitive sentiments therein. One has to imagine it because, usually, it's dictated by geometric and calculated pressure for some therapeutic reconciliation – confines that protect both parties from the space you're seeking. You can't get there without some red temptation. That space isn't imposing itself if some part of you isn't thoroughly rallying a coup, requiring all of the Zen and forebrain you can summon to deny it. It's not the sex that'll get there – it's the refusal to submit.

Or, just a step further, one can be honest. It's a near-unrivaled invitation into mutual solipsism. And, perhaps, the most useful of its virtues is its propensity to bring about the only more rigorous invitation.

Ghosts

He paced between the couch and the window, staring at his phone screen, then opened the window to let in the breeze. Kneeling by the couch, he angled a cushion upright and beat it to death. Words wouldn't come out. *A little after 2pm*. A bold ambition overtook him, and he marched towards the bathroom.

He shut the door hard behind him and reached through the shower curtain, pulling the hot water knob out and twisting it all the way left, allowing the pressure and heat to build. He slithered out of his clothes and tossed them to the floor, as behind the curtain the water had warmed. He stepped in and swung his head under the water to soak his hair and body, then reached for shampoo and body wash, scrubbing everywhere ferociously. Rinsing felt numb. He pushed the knob back into the wall, pulled open the curtain and reached for a towel, tossing and toiling his mop of hair until it was barely damp before stepping out.

As the fog in his mirror cleared, he caught his frame in it. He didn't look like how little he'd been eating.

To his bedroom. From the top drawer of an old wood chest, he pulled out a pair of black underwear, one of some twenty identical pairs. In the next drawer down, he found a long black t-shirt – one of twenty identical. The bottom drawer held light-wash jeans –only one pair of those. He pulled them each over himself, then slunk to the closet to retrieve his favorite baggy, maroon sweater.

He emerged, to any eyes that might intercept him, looking very much alive.

Down the block, the Coffee Bean hardly resembled what 3:30 looks like anywhere else. Dozens of gainfully employed were flooding in and out on their breaks, some occupying the high-top tables. The neon-red sign above the door flashed as it slowly died. He thought twice about the need to interact with such a busy place but had made such an effort to leave that turning back would become an irreconcilable failure. A troupe of eager cappuccino drinkers nodded silently as he held the door for them.

Inside, a line of five or six ghostly figures stood between him and his tea. He nearly rolled his eyes as he got in line. They all ordered complicated iced coffees and smoothies that took several minutes apiece to serve. The line halted for each. He gazed over the people ahead of him, then at the wall of coffee beans for take-home, then at the menu – never considering something besides his unsweet iced green tea – then at the baristas, decisive and quick as they desperately filled the convoluted orders ahead of him.

"Can I have a mocha latte? Dash of heavy cream?" a mousy voice rose in front.

"Is that all?"

"Mmm. Thank you."

"Have a good one," the barista said.

"Thank you. You too."

He turned to absorb the figure of the ghost speaking. She was little, olive skin and wavy brown hair, and her voice was suspiciously smooth – two orders ahead. He couldn't see her face. He nearly said aloud, "Thank you for your simple order."

At last, he ordered his tea. James behind the counter had begun filling it before he finished ordering.

"How's it going, man?"

"Not sure if it is, truthfully."

"Heh. Work going okay?"

He shrugged. "Some days, trying hard today."

"Glad to see it, man. Here ya go." James handed him the extra-large tea.

"Thank you, sir, always a pleasure."

"Indeed," James said. James appreciated the speed with which small talk could be accomplished. James cared.

He reached for his tea, pulled a straw from their cup on the counter, tore its wrapper away, jammed it into his tea through a pile of ice, and gulped half of it down in an instant.

There was nowhere to sit. Individuals occupied all the tables for two, as custom dictated. He adjusted the bag over his shoulder before it slipped and spotted a single opening in the whole place – at the lone table for four, where the latte ghost had sat.

He was in no mood to exchange another word with anybody but kept scanning the impossibly busy Coffee Bean to no avail. *This country needs siestas – so all of these people could take an hour off and leave me to claim a table in peace.*

"Do you mind?" he said in defeat.

"No, go ahead." She gestured to the empty space across from hers.

"Thank you."

He pulled a notebook and his favorite pen from his bag and dropped the bag to the floor. He slid over the seat diagonal from her, took another swig of tea, opened to a fresh page, and clicked the pen.

> The café was impossibly full – a drag to be
> reckoned with. NO. JUNK.

He pulled himself out from that mind, clearly not working yet. He started to write lazy political thoughts, and resounding accusations of treason flooded three pages quickly, before he leaned over his notebook, face in hands, and started pulling hard at his hair. Fuck the purposelessness of the words that came the most easily.

"Struggling?"

He looked up. "Hmm?"

"Seems like you're having a hard time." She grinned meanly.

He snickered at himself. "Yeah, it's not going well."

He couldn't let her see how intently he was studying her face. She had high cheeks, dark eyes, hardly any makeup on

49

but a trace of eyeliner. He'd just begun peripherally tracing her lips when—

"You shouldn't force it."

"Probably not, but what else would I do?"

"Ah, so you're a *real* writer," she grinned.

"What does that mean?"

"It means…you give a shit." She eyed him sideways to make clear her jest.

"That's offering much too much credit."

"I don't think so. You've nearly pulled all your hair out over it."

"Well, if I weren't a little masochistic, I'd have gone into something more grounded. Like government." He planted his elbows on the table and his head up at her.

"Well, just try not to hurt yourself too bad too fast."

"No promises," he smiled. "What are you working on?"

She had her nose glued to the inner binding of a textbook and a pair of headphones over her hair, only covering her right ear.

"Reading some awful old poetry for class."

He copied her one-sided smirk. "My sympathies."

"Thank you."

"What are you studying?"

"Writing," she said proudly, gaze back in her book.

"Do you have to?" He rolled his eyes.

"Yeah, it's what I want to do. Well, some of it."

"Are you sure?"

"Yes." She scratched her shoulder through her t-shirt.

"Really?"

Shepherd

"Mmm."

"Are you *sure* you're sure?"

"Very." The beds of her fingernails were all torn up, much like his. She brought the hand that wasn't cradling her book to her lips, fed herself the edge of her thumb, and nibbled on it slowly, her focus shifting between the nail and his expression.

He had to unlatch his eyes again. "Damn."

"What?"

"Well, I just hate to see good people walking into the incinerator."

Her laugh was hearty, long-winded, and never put on.

"Especially if you're good. I don't need more competition."

"Oh, so you're competitive?"

"What else gave it away?"

"How fast you got those pages done," she eyed the notebook under his hand. He'd all but forgotten it.

"What are you listening to?" he asked.

"Simon and Garfunkel."

Good. "Which song?"

"*Kathy's.*"

"Wow, tremendous."

"Thank you." She was as quick and as terse as he would suggest.

They paused for her to study him as he had her.

"Is that your favorite?" he finally continued, folding his arms.

Her head was buried again. "No."

"Which—"

51

"*Scarborough*, if I had to choose." The effort to look back at him would only be spared for very special questions and answers.

"Interesting. I wouldn't have thought."

"I love their medieval-sounding songs."

Wow. First he was quiet and then, "*Barbriallen.*"

"*Rose of Aberdeen*," she fired back.

"*The Side of a Hill.*"

She nodded. ". Nice. The best."

"What poem are you reading?" he asked.

"Wordsworth. Kind of terrible?"

"Enormously." While she laughed, he pretended a nervous look-around. "Shh – don't tell anyone I said that."

"Who do you like?" she wondered while he spoke.

"I doubt you'd agree."

She shrugged. "Try me."

"Thomas Wyatt." He squinted, bracing for a tease or a slap.

"Wow."

"What?"

"Well, that's definitely unexpected. A little lame."

"Dramatic?" he asked.

With a huff, she closed her book and leaned forward. "Just a little."

He cracked his knuckles, weary of the perilous risks of being lame. "Yuck."

"No, it's cool," she said, resting her chin on her fist.

"That's definitely too kind of you."

"Maybe," she recycled the mean grin.

"That's a 'yes,'" he said.

"Well, what are *you* working on?"

"A cumbersome tome that I'll probably never finish."

"Intriguing," she deepened her voice in parody of all meters serious. "What's it about?"

He copied her expression again. "Hmm. It's about a long series of regrets, failing to drink them away, the usual."

"Sounds like you need to drink less and write more."

"That's the plan."

"Good."

"Thank you."

He stared at her a while. "Hmm."

"What?"

"Nothing."

They returned to their books.

After a few minutes, a series of loud, deep scratching sounds sprang from his notebook, and a moment later, he brought it down hard and angrily to the tabletop with both hands, letting out a "Dammit!"

"What's wrong?"

"Everything is junk."

"I'm sure it's not junk," she said quietly, in case she was wrong. Her head didn't move.

"No, really – I don't know why I bother."

"You should quit then."

Nice, she's not biting. "I can't."

"I know."

"Haha. Thank you again."

"Don't mention it." She found the time on the phone and straightened her posture. "Aw, shit, I have to be going. Class."

"Damn."

"Well, it was a pleasure talking to you," the shrug, again.

"All mine."

"Hmm, maybe," she mocked with another sideways smirk.

"No arguments here," he laughed.

"You should put up more of a fight, then."

"Me? Never."

"Well, I'll see you around." The ghost glided from the table in one smooth motion.

"I'm sure." *Please.*

"Mmm."

He was silent, off guard, bettered; he retreated into his notebook not to reveal it. It was all very confusing. The wires were tangled, the lines were crossed: she was infinitely quicker and cooler than he was. And by the time he realized he didn't know her name, she was nearing the door and already a thousand miles away and for all he knew gone back to whichever ethereal plane she came from. And the words to *Kathy's Song* repeated to him as she took her name and number and walked out of the Coffee Bean.

Cast a Stone

"So, let me get this straight: you accidentally sat next to a woman at the coffee shop who was literally *exactly* the same as you, but also funny and very nice, and you talked for a long time and worked next to her – which you *never* do – and you didn't get her phone number?"

"That's correct." He sat in his desk chair, the layers of laundry previously occupying it hurled to his bed and listened to Christopher rage over speakerphone.

"You know, I've long suspected that I might be dumber than you are – oh, not in matters of logic, perhaps, but certainly in social things." A pause. The sound of Christopher winding up. "But *that*... That may, in fact, be the stupidest thing I've ever heard of."

He laughed. "Well, don't worry, *fiend*, you are undoubtedly the *dumbest* socialite out there. I'm not coming for your title."

55

Christopher calmed himself before continuing the interrogation. "But, seriously, how could you not even attempt—"

"Because I wasn't *trying* to get her number. I wasn't trying to flirt with her. I just enjoyed our conversation. It brought me back to life a little bit."

"You never got her name, either?"

"Nothing. Maybe I'll never see her again." He'd already fantasized about it.

"What's the matter with you?"

"You know, fool, not every relationship had with women, by men, ought to be forged with the spectrum of chivalry and the range of carnality in mind."

Christopher scoffed on command. "Seemingly. In theory."

"You're outrageous."

"No. Even if you were just looking for a friend and enjoyed her company, why would you not ask for her name? And I still don't believe you on the first count, by the way."

"I was all wrapped up in conversation," he stuttered. "It was locked outside time. It didn't seem like what happened after mattered, and then it was over, and I didn't think or even care to ask."

"You're an in*sane* person."

"And on the first count, I don't know what to tell you. It meant so much to have a conversation with a stranger that was not only pleasant, but engaging and thorough. She was just a placeholder. A pair of pliers for me to pull myself out of the decaying wood," he rifled through the thought trying to believe it.

Hardly concealing his irritation, Christopher kept it up. "You can pepper up your explanation however you like, fool, but you felt something, and regret not finding out more."

"I do regret not finding out more, but only insofar as I cannot have another nice conversation. And not more than I enjoy the thought of never seeing her again."

"You're seriously going to sit here and tell me you aren't attracted to someone you describe as 'incredibly witty and smart,' and 'interested in all the right things?'"

"I am, and I am also rather disappointed in your surprising propensity to think a man cannot take interest in a woman in any measure that's not romantic or physical," he teased.

Christopher was no misogynist, but he amused himself however convenient. "Perhaps you've sterilized yourself in the last few months, and that's why you're suddenly a Buddhist."

"I'm almost offended, *knave*," he said. "I've always fancied myself rather Zen. I'm telling you: I wasn't into her. I just liked her. As a person. You know, in the whole time I've known you, I've haven't met many new people to like."

"Well, that's not their faults. Who could compare to me?"

"Caligula, evidently."

"Ha!"

"Besides, Christopher," Christopher did not like hyphenated or bastardized forms of his name, even from him, "I still miss Sara very much, and if I'm being honest…"

"Let me stop you right there. I'm not sure I ever want to hear you speaking honestly."

He forced a lazy chuckle. "Outrageous."

"What? I may not be Pinocchio, but I'm taller laying down."

"Christ. Well, sorry. I was just going to say —"

Christopher interrupted, "If you were *just going to say* it, you wouldn't be about to say it right now."

"What are you, me?"

"No, I'm much, much better than you."

"I was just going to say that I still miss Sara, and I'm essentially non-functional without her, and I'm most certainly not interested in talking to anybody else."

"I figured."

"Penny called me the other day," he said, not sure where to start.

"And in what way did she provide you sufficient means of deflection for this moment?"

"Very good. Well, she first offered to introduce me to a friend of hers, whom she said is 'just my type' and is 'very pretty,' to which I kindly rephrased, 'get the fuck out of here.'"

"Good use of 'whom,' though." Christopher applauded.

Christopher knew, better than most people, the difference between 'who' and 'whom.' In fact, between the two of them, the financier knew it better than the author. Many things were that way.

"Yes, at least she provided me with that. And then, thinking herself more subtle than she was, she asked me 'not to' tell Si that he should quit twiddling his thumbs and propose already."

"Jesus."

"Yeah."

Christopher laughed. "Insidious."

"Yep."

"And what did you tell her?"

"You first." He'd been suspecting himself not the only target of Penny's plan.

"How did you know?"

"I haven't heard back from her yet, so I figured she had asked us both to put on the pressure and see which one did first."

With a satisfied sigh, Christopher recounted, "I told her I would 'of course not' reveal it to Si and proceeded to *actually* not reveal it to Si."

"Ha. I did the same. I did, however, write about it, and it's very funny."

"That's grand. So, she provided at least two items then, unwittingly."

"She did. Unfortunately, with the wedding approaching, it won't be the last we hear of this. I'm worried that Si is actually going to make that move," he said.

"Yeah. It's just a matter of time now."

"I don't think it's bad. Penny's great. Most girlfriends wouldn't bother getting so close with us, you know?"

"Hmph," Christopher muttered, "No, most wouldn't make that mistake."

"No, they wouldn't. So, what has us each spooked, if not her?"

"Well, if Si hasn't asked her by now, he doesn't plan to for even longer – and if he suddenly does because of the pressure from Alyssa's and Cody's wedding—"

He piped in, "Nice use of the correct plural, 'Alyssa's and Cody's.'"

"Thank you." Christopher didn't miss a beat, "And if he suddenly does because of the pressure from Alyssa's and Cody's wedding, it wouldn't be his choice and could lead to resentment and not the best marriage."

He thought for a while. "Is it that, or are we worried about how often we'll ever see Si again."

"Ah. Right. That's the one. Anyway, you are lying to me about that girl, and you are a serious fool for it. And an even more serious fool – like, a fool so foolish I worry for your safety as you cross the road – for not finding out her name or her number."

"If I never see her again, it'll be a nice conversation I'll forget about."

"Could have been a nice date you'd forget about," Christopher said.

He cracked his knuckles loud enough for the phone. "You need unprofessional help."

"That's why I talk to you."

"You don't realize I've been charging by the hour all these years."

"What're we up to now?"

"You know that yacht we're getting for the bachelor party?" he said.

"Yeah," Christopher said.

"If I decide I like it a lot, you may as well buy it for me, and we'll call it even."

"Ha! That's a bit steep, no?"

He balked. "Nothing's too steep for you, the way I hear."

"That'd be true if I hadn't been to the casino every weekend for the last two months."

"You'd better start saving up for my yacht, then."

Christopher answered with the fake chuckle and one of his 'a-hAs.' "Perhaps. Alright, I'll speak to you later. You're a fool."

"Yep. You're a heathen."

Late into the evening, too tired to censor his rambling, he raced through the pages of an unidentifiable scene, unwilling to decide who it was about.

> I sat across from her, sipping my iced tea, fidgeting to get comfortable in my barstool, afraid we were about to have it out in a Starbucks. I'd have preferred a walk outside or a long drive – something more peaceful, more reminiscent of our first few important talks.
>
> She brushed her wavy blonde hair to the side, only for it to slide right back in her way; her sharp blue eyes glued to me, as if she was

excavating through whatever contortions my face twisted, for clues or remnants of a distant past, once the highlight of each conversation, now forgotten except in these sorts of moments – when we'd figure out if we were still anything or if it was well and truly time to emigrate to a new civilization. She gulped down more of her cold brew, which had had about fourteen flavors added, and began to stare.

She preferred this be done in Starbucks. And that was the greatest contortion of all, I thought: I had always made of all these moments whatever it was she wanted. I never had been so much the subordinate – never of the inferior will – but it mattered deeply to me that, if she needed some anchor to justice and decent persuasion, I should provide it, whatever my distaste, and never stand against it. And in becoming that passive rock, I had forgone my own inclinations often enough that she'd begun to accuse me of having none – of being less a man. I had realized then that she was the flighty one, and I the stone. I had not truly changed form, and she was guided up the road and back by each passing breeze.

Her skinny frame gathered some new strength from the coffee, and finally began, "So, how are you?"

We had not spoken for several weeks – a new custom, an effort to regain our senses of self, some fresh air. In that time, I had reconsidered my willingness to endure it, and every suggestion of goodwill now seemed suspicious and selfish at best.

I laughed lightly to show that pain without accusation, "I'm hanging in there," I said delicately. I wasn't trying to fool her, only to show her what it was all doing to me. "And you?"

"I'm fine," she said decidedly, either triumphant or spiteful, or both. She never used to be spiteful.

"What have you been up to?" we both said at once, before chuckling at our learned sameness. Perhaps in the previous weeks she had unraveled the compulsions of that sameness, finding it hollow and loose-fitting, as I had come to suspect.

"You first," I said.

"Alright," she took a deep breath, another long gulp of cold brew, and exhaled, "I'm doing well," she was attentive, but chuckled again.

"Good, that's good," I answered, as the sincerity on her end of this talk was confronted for the first time by the half-heartedness I would need to survive. "What have you been up to?"

She seemed to hope that I'd take over more then, but I had known that before asking.

"Well," she began slowly, as if she hadn't known with what she'd filled her time the last two months, instead of me, "I've been writing a lot, working with some friends. Just so busy with work. And we have an outline of the show now…"

"Hey, that's awesome!" I interjected.

"Thank you. So, yeah, I've just been doing stuff every day and having lots of new ideas; it feels really nice," she wasn't having much difficulty implying how well she got along without me though she had difficulty doing it subtly. "And besides that, I've just been working out a lot."

Readily I answered, "That's wonderful; do you feel well?" No amount of time might pass that I could neglect to ask of her chronically achy joints and trouble eating and so on.

She smiled as she answered, "Yeah, I feel good. I've been eating mostly vegan, drinking only water...I feel great," and she was glowing. No one would say otherwise. For all my efforts at the gym and in my diet, I still presented as a lowly worm, perhaps a bit smaller, but who could tell? I certainly couldn't. She had a cycle of "new" diets she'd employ every few months, and within days of the change would lose ten pounds and feel completely alive. I had a cycle of trying to eat less and work out more, with which I was successful about sixty percent of the time, and the net was neutral. In fairness, the weeks leading up to this meeting were often fraught with food or drink that took the place of her company, so at least to me, my standstill was understood.

She let loose her waiting retort, "So, how are you? Really?"

"I'm alright," I fumbled out, "I've been working out five or six times a week at least, eating pretty well. I've been writing a lot more, just by necessity, and I'm glad to reclaim some of my powers," I overemphasized here and there for a laugh. She obliged. "The palpitations have come back, though, and I've noticed they don't always get better when I work out."

She interrupted fast, "Oh, you poor thing, you have to see the doctor about that."

I wasn't sure how to interpret the phrase "you poor thing," and immediately became more anxious about that than anything else I had ever heard, and I responded,

"Yeah, if it persists another few days I'm going to. I'm just hoping it's stress, and it'll subside anytime now."

"Well, you have to make sure you're careful; that's not something to mess around with," she insisted.

"Yeah, I'm taking it seriously, don't worry. But thank you."

"Of course," she said especially reassuringly.

So, we came to new and discomforting territory, having caught up. Next, we had to address our great matter, and the pleasantries of the preceding few minutes hadn't exactly cauterized us for the danger. Neither she nor I wanted to shift towards such uneven ground.

As a long moment of silence overcame us, I reviewed the ways we spoke. I liked to slither through thoughts, never racing directly at them, but never forfeiting a detail or a turn of phrase; she was a charging rhino, slowly walking before engaging, building up worry and forethought, then stampeding through it. She was here, I had already feared, either to end things for good or to apologize for the fact that she still needed more time apart. There was no need for a sit-down if the news was any better. And, despite that frightening range of outcomes, she had run straight through my questionable health, back into a place of sensitive presence and fear – investment, even.

At the least, I thought, I should show her that after this time alone, I would direct us, given the chance.

"So, if I may," I began—

"Yes?" she answered, coyly.

I smirked at her. "So, you obviously feel great and have been doing really well, and I'm really proud of you."

"Thank you," she said, dry and quippy, teasing the outline of my eventual question by predicting it. She knew, of course, that I didn't like leaving the big questions for the end – the anxiousness and curiosity were indefatigable.

"Of course," I said. "So, I have to ask, do you find yourself happier? What exactly do you want us to do, us to be?" She was silent for a while, so I continued, "Because I have to admit, it's really hard for me. I'm still happy and willing to do this because my goal is the same. But it's not easy. And I'm sorry to say that because it's not just about me."

I counted the seconds before she said something out of character, something to the effect, "There you go, always saying sorry for your feelings," or some such post-modern psychological nonsense.

But she didn't. She was silent for a few more moments, and then answered, "I'm sorry it's hard. But this is just something I need to do. You know I love you, but I really...Too much has happened. I'm just completely shut down. I can't feel romantic, I can't be physical, I can't do any of it. I just need to be alone."

"I know, and I get it. I don't have a problem with this. I was just curious how you felt now compared to before," I said, trying to steer us away from the most dramatic of problems.

"I feel better," she said. "I do feel better, I'm just not ready to go back. I just don't feel like myself or like I can be loving right now," somehow, the same thought transposed onto new words always found new ways to crush me.

This was our way. She would decide how we carried on, and I would endure. And this was perfectly alright. If I had the fortitude, I should wait around for the woman I love. It didn't mean I was weak, or I was unwilling to choose myself over anything else. It meant I was willing to do whatever it took as long as I wound up with her in the end. There was goodness in that, there was honor. Truth be told, I relished the suffering. It was the closest to chivalry I could get, I thought.

I answered, "Yes, I understand," and said nothing else.

"I'm sorry," she offered gently. "This is just what I have to do. And I know how hard it is for you."

"It's alright," I mumbled again. She was looking at me like I was a scared turtle, my shell a protective layer of patience. Before she could offer more condolences, which only rang hollower the longer she distanced herself from me, I retraced, "So, tell me more about how the show is looking. What kind of episode plots are you thinking about, what's the season one arc?"

She paused for a moment, deciding whether to take the bait and forgo our status. Maybe she just felt guilty enough to leave it aside for my wellbeing.

"So, season one is about the main character joining the team of writers and meeting all these people and all the crazy, behind-the-scenes shit."

We continued for a while like this, exchanging our latest, setting aside the past and the future; she hoping the distraction would make me feel better, and I that it would make her feel more in love with me. There was never really any hope for either. She just needed the time I didn't have.

Suddenly, after maybe an hour, she picked up her phone and announced, "Oh no, I have a meeting at two-fifteen."

"Oh," I said, "You've got to get moving then."

"Yeah, I'm sorry," she said. I passed no judgment of her repeated apologies. "It was great to catch up with you," she said, as if to some old acquaintance.

Shepherd

Shortly, I said back, "Yeah, you too."

"I'll call you," she said, gathering her purse and her empty cold brew cup.

"Okay, I'm always here," I said, trying to inject some reminder of what I was supposed to mean to her.

"I know," she said.

We hugged and she left, and I took my time leaving. I couldn't believe she had used Han's line against me – and she didn't even know it. She had never watched Empire with me.

71

Bachelor Hour

Ultimately, the musings and motives of women are,
we all know, impossible to infiltrate or to grasp.

He pulled a grey duffle bag from his jacket closet and stuffed it with socks, underwear, t-shirts, jeans, and two folded black dress shirts. Among his clothes he planted a card filled with cash, another roll of cash, a cheap Indiana Jones fedora from a Halloween costume, its matching bullwhip, toiletries, and two bottles of Johnny Walker. More, he was sure, would be procured in Boston.

"Have you got everything?" Christopher asked.

He had the phone wedged between his chin and shoulder. "Yes. Have you got everything set?"

"Getting there." Christopher sounded stressed. He would most often absorb the brunt of his anxiety without outwardly expressing it – but the task list for Cody's surprise bachelor party was especially taxing. While the rest of the guests drove and rode trains from all over the east coast, Christopher, the only resident of the city less Cody himself, had to check the hotel, the restaurant, and the yacht in advance. Eight of them would later convene at the yacht, having fetched supplies of booze and nosh, and Christopher would lead Cody to the docks, chosen for the convenience that they were unsuspectingly next door to a watering hole the two of them frequented.

"Who do you think shows up late and ruins the entire thing?" he wondered.

"Mike," Christopher had already thought.

"Ugh. Mike. Barely know the guy. Why was he invited?"

"Alyssa said these guys would all be offended if they weren't invited."

"That sounds like a 'Cody-and-Alyssa problem,'" he said.

"Yes, it does. And yet…"

"And yet we're stuck with them."

Christopher sounded out of breath – he was halfway along the harbor scouting out sights for later. "On second thought, not Mike."

"Not Mike?"

"Mike is a weirdo-cretin who has no business being there but actually seems to understand that. He just doesn't want us to throw him off the boat. I think he'll be early."

"Fair. Franky?" he suggested.

"Franky's the opposite," Christopher explained, stopping to rest." If anything – he's so sure of himself and how much everyone loves him that he won't risk damaging the reputation he's wrong about having by being late."

He laughed, zipping his bag and slumping down on the edge of his bed. "Sure. Plus, he's into nearly *all* of Alyssa's

73

friends and doesn't want the rest of the wedding party angry at him."

"But, if he ruined the bachelor party, the bridesmaids would probably applaud that."

"Ah," he said with a rich, Victorian sigh. "True. Okay, let's put an asterisk on Franky. I'll call him from the train once I'm out in the open later to check on him."

"I think it'll be Joey," Christopher said.

"Really? I got the impression Joey was really excited."

"Sure, but he's the least invested in Cody and lives the farthest away besides you."

"Taking the Vegas odds, huh?"

"That's how I win all my money."

He smirked. "Just not recently."

"Hey…"

They laughed loudly, which, for Christopher, was meant to show the passersby how *happening* their situation was.

"By the way, do you have the cash on hand to buy my new yacht during this excursion?" he reminded.

"Nope. But I might by the time we get through with the poker game."

"You might."

Picking up speed and breathing again, Christopher said with a huff, "I still can't believe you wouldn't let any women be involved in these festivities."

"Even if Alyssa wasn't sure to neuter you all for doing that at Co's bachelor party, I'd never allow anything so unchivalrous and so cliché to go down on my watch."

"You're just so prim and proper, aren't you?"

"Once again, we're confronted by the challenge you and the rest of them seem to find in respecting women," he laughed with himself, standing and throwing his bag over his non-phone shoulder.

"Hey, I respect women," Christopher said, a bit loudly.

They paused, waiting for the next move.

After too long, he said, "Oh, sorry, I thought you were about to add a qualifier. Because you don't respect women."

"God. Seriously, I'm calling Cody. Talk to me when you're on the train. And fuck off."

Between laughs, he accused, "Fool. Hooligan – *Fooligan*."

> *Poker isn't the best card game because it's all about lying for reward; it's the best card* game because it reveals two things: how seriously everyone around the table takes a challenge, and who's a stylish competitor. It's not just a psychological competition, a measurement of cards passed by, a war of patience and subtlety, deception, and redirection – it's a reveal. It's the alcohol of games. It doesn't disguise someone's person, it reveals it. A tried and slow-burning player can unravel the truths of their competitors without opening his own mouth. And, having discovered the truth, a particularly smart player can keep his mouth shut even longer and steal all the other guy's money.

Naturally, once the party had boarded the yacht, and a few outliers climbed to the top deck to sightsee through the harbor and the coastline, the rest gathered below deck for a high-stakes, timed session of Hold-Em. Three hours. A grand per man to play. No limit bets. Winner-take-all for the man with the most chips remaining when time ran out. He and Christopher had a decade of hustling private games together under their belts. They had hand and eye signals figured out, each counted the cards, and were more experienced than most of the table at fair play to boot. On Cody's special occasion, with the groom-to-be sitting at the table, they decided to put away their tricks and play fair.

And then they decided not to.

All afternoon, en route to the yacht, over initial cocktails and toasts, and through introductions from Captain Don – a very nice man, halfway between a pirate and Don Draper – Franky and Joey, a pair of out-of-town distant friends of Cody's, who were not members of the wedding party and were only invited as a courtesy, had interrupted everything. Their tasteless, rude, stupid remarks had seriously dragged on the first wave of festivities, and they could not be allowed to get away with it. The rest of the party at the table would have to bear the weight of retribution too.

Christopher started small. He used undetectable ticks to indicate his own cards and those that had passed. They both read and bluffed the conservative players out of every hand, time and again, collecting small grabs and buffering their risk as it grew. When aggressive players – a camp to which both Franky and Joey belonged – would not be bluffed out, they wagered low, got the others to commit, doubled down, and took them big. The rest of them were slow played out of the game – seldom winning their own hands. The big betters won a few small hands early and were soon ripped away from their fortunes. He and Christopher were the last in play, and, as a gentlemanly custom, agreed to split the ten-thousand-dollar winnings fifty-fifty. They were paragons of courtesy.

"You guys are absurd," Cody took him aside after to whisper. "I know what you pulled; you do that every time."

They stood at the stern, a clear breeze brushing against the backs of their necks while the other gentlemen overdrank above and below.

"What are you talking about?" he asked, his acting good enough for anyone but Cody.

"You guys just hustled eight grand off that table without breaking a sweat, and I want my thousand back, plus another two, to keep my mouth shut."

"Co, I have no idea what you're talking about. Christopher and I are the most experienced players at the table – it's not really surprising that we'd win, is it?"

Cody cocked an eyebrow and contorted his mouth in a diagonal. "Come on."

"You really think I'd do that at your bachelor party?"

"Three thousand more."

He sighed. "Fine. We'll talk to him afterwards. I'm not putting it all up myself."

"Thought so," Cody smiled to himself.

"How'd you know?" he said.

"I didn't; now I do."

He laughed. "Very clever – but you must have suspected if you took the gamble of accusing."

Cody's smiling hadn't moved. "I knew you wouldn't be offended. I've seen you take more."

"Fair enough. Three back to you it is."

"Four."

"Four," he agreed without pause. "Let's have a drink, eh?"

"Good doing business with you." Cody reached out a hand and they shook.

They toasted Cody's wedding – and silently toasted their profiteering.

Christopher approached.

"I'll be back in a bit," Cody said, hurrying off to hear Captain Don joke about his ex-wife.

"Was it something I said?" Christopher muttered as Cody passed without comment.

"No, he just didn't want to be the one to tell you that we have to give him four grand from our earnings to keep him quiet."

"God fucking dammit. You let him get away with that?"

"Yes and no. I mean, yes, I did let him; no to your follow-up question."

"He didn't trick you?" Christopher asked.

"Just thought it was a nice additional gift from us. Can't hurt our stock with Alyssa for the next few decades if we helped with the down payment on their place."

"Excellent. We may, yet, ever see *him* again, at least."

"Indeed."

"Gents?" Simon took his turn in their inner circle by the stern.

Christopher stifled a nervous hop and addressed him casually, "Hey, Si, what's happening?."

Simon toasted at nothing in particular with his drink. Facing the bay, he swooned in place, unable to focus on one object. "So, I'm thinking Pen's going to want me to propose soon."

"Oh yeah?"

"Yeah," Simon said anxiously, "I can tell she's getting impatient. I don't know – I want to, ya know? I was just hoping we'd have more time to…"

"Keep going like this," Christopher finished.

"Yeah." Simon bowed his head.

He searched for the right kind of encouragement. "It's alright, man. Just do what feels right, I guess. If you want to anyway, just roll with it." There was no sense in losing with Simon the progress they'd just made with Cody. "I mean, it's not like everyone doesn't expect it."

"Sure," Simon muttered, "But, you know, I like how things are. And it changes. I mean, look at him." He pointed at Cody on the top deck, looking only halfheartedly brightened by all his closest friends. "You get so that nothing besides her makes you feel whole."

He smiled. "Yeah, I guess so."

Still searching for something to look at, Simon waved his arms back and forth and raised his voice. "And that's great, it's just…No matter how much I love her, I'm not there yet."

"Nobody really is," he said, "You just do it and try to enjoy it."

"Yeah, what're you complaining to the pair of us about it for?" Christopher said. "What, we're single after *how long*? And you and Cody come around, all 'poor me, with my beautiful girlfriend, or fiancé, ugh, how do you guys *do it*?!'"

Simon and he snickered.

"Sorry, you know what I mean. Ah. Whatever. Anyway, just wanted to broach the subject with you both. You know, in case it happens soon."

"Thanks, man. Yeah, let us know," he said.

Simon rejoined the others, and he and Christopher raised their glasses, rolling their eyes and grinning.

Over dinner, Joey and Franky were as boisterous as ever. They flirted with the servers, the bartender, and even the manager of the small Italian restaurant that their party occupied half of. It was hellishly embarrassing. The drunkenness and stupidity had washed over the lot of them a few hours earlier than expected.

"I'm so sorry about this," he said to the server who'd been tending to their half of the table. "Even though it's a bachelor party, we didn't know those two would be such trouble."

"That's okay, hun, I know it's not you. Another glass?"

"When you can – please, take your time. Thanks."

As she walked away, Franky loudly spit across the long table, "Hey, sweethaht, you wanna grab me anothah glass too? And while you're at it, we're staying at the Hilton—"

Christopher interrupted, "If you don't shut your fucking mouth, Franky, you're not staying anywhere. Miss, we're very sorry. Please don't bother bringing that clown a drink. Franky, let's step outside."

Once they were outside, the noise in the restaurant revived, he took up a glass, "Christopher!" The rest of them laughed and toasted.

After dinner, he raised his sixth or seventh of the day – he couldn't recall – and began to toast: "Cody, my dear old friend. Soon, you'll be taking a huge step forward. We couldn't be prouder of you. You're marrying a wonderful girl who's been nothing but kind and friendly and fun to all of us, we're lucky to have her in our lives and that you'll be enriched by her. So, before we retreat for the evening, I'd actually like to toast Alyssa. You all know we love Co. Let's have a great night, fellas."

The table cheered, and so did some of the other guests. They guzzled another round and began to clean up and head for the door.

"Thanks man," Cody said privately as they walked to their hotel. "That was great. She really loves you too, man. We're so happy you're in the wedding."

"And I'm honored, man. It's gonna be a blast, and a wonderful life." The ratio he'd prescribed for the outing was one earnest line for every drink.

Cody stretched his arms. "I'll drink to that."

"And mostly anything else."

"You're not wrong." They clinked again, this time a pair of hidden bottles of scotch in paper bags as they led a platoon of drunkards down Charles Street.

Upon entering their suite, the group discovered it had been renovated. It had become a puzzle room. Maps, clues, false doors, and hidden items led them from one bedroom to the next, unlocking prizes and drinks and desserts. When they reached the final room, a host of liquor, psychedelics, and more games awaited them.

"Who did this?" Cody pestered over and over through the night. "This is unreal."

Neither he nor Christopher took credit. Everybody knew.

The group settled into the suite. Some played games, some drank more and threatened to call hookers – which resulted in Christopher being deployed to physically threaten them – and some indulged in impressive doses of mushrooms and herbs, among other things.

Whatever happened after that, he didn't know. He locked himself in his bedroom and drank more. He thought about Sara. A knock came from the door.

"What're you doing in there? Come on out! It's crazy!" He couldn't tell which idiot was talking.

A heavier knock followed a few minutes later. "Are you alright?" It wasn't a question.

He was near to blacking out, he could feel. He rose from the bed and pulled the door open gingerly. Everything spun. "I'm great. Hanging in there. How are you?"

"Get out of here, guys, go hang. I'll speak to him," Christopher shooed away three or four tertiary guys. He entered and closed the door behind him. They sat on the floor of the off-white, carpeted room across from one another. "What's happening?"

"Who cares, man? Jesus Christ, who cares?"

Christopher scolded in a half whisper, "You put together a big, beautiful, fabulous party for all these fools and you're not enjoying it, that's what's happening."

"I put it together for Cody, not them, not me. So did you."

"Well, I sort of did it for me…"

"Ha! Very good." He trailed off and Christopher didn't laugh.

"What is it?"

He waved Christopher off. "Come on, are you going to make me spill all my secrets when I'm too drunk to stand?"

"If that's the only time they'll pour out."

He waited in silence for a minute or two. "I haven't slept through the night in months. I'm drinking a lot, day and night. I've written nothing worth keeping since September. I don't enjoy being alive."

"Well, that really gets at the heart of the issue, doesn't it?" Christopher said.

"Yep."

They cackled.

"Seriously, about the new book, why are you having trouble?"

"Because I'm writing about Sara, and I feel guilty about that, and it's hard to write about."

"It's not that hard to write about. You've written about it before."

"Not like this," he said. "Not so personally. Not so close."

"Then don't do that now. Wait until it's a distant memory."

"Then it won't be as good." He sipped on a half-empty nip of scotch.

"Well, fucking pick one, dickhead."

"I'm trying so hard to pick anything."

Christopher sighed his long, dramatic sigh. "What else are you writing about?"

"How hard it is to write."

"Well, you've got plenty of material about that."

"No, I don't…"

They cackled again.

"Seriously, do you feel like you have a problem?" Christopher said.

"I have a problem with not writing enough."

"You know what I mean."

He shrugged. "I know what you mean, and I have little enough of a problem that I'm deflecting your question with a shallow, unfunny joke."

"That sounds like a more substantial problem to me."

"Well, it's not one – but thank you anyway." He finished the tiny bottle and threw it violently against the undecorated wall, hoping to elicit a laugh that was not forthcoming.

"What are you going to do about your book?"

"What do you mean?"

"I mean, they want it, right? At this rate, it's going to be late."

"February."

"And you don't care about that?" Christopher raised his voice.

"It's funny, actually. I *do* care about that – but I care so little about anything else that it's hard to focus more than a few seconds per day on how much I care about that."

"So, what are you going to do?"

"Write the book, which I'm trying to do."

"If you can't finish it before they give up on you?"

"They won't give up on me." *Oh, they most certainly will.*

"Why not?"

"What are you going to say, 'Sara gave up on you, so readers and publishers will, too'?"

Christopher pity-laughed. "That's not what I was going to say."

"Well, I'm going to finish the thing when I know what it is and when I can bring myself to do it. It's not like I haven't been trying."

"I know that. But you know you're struggling. This is a real concern. This is your livelihood. You just spent however many thousands on this weekend. It's great of you to do that, really, it is. But what are you going to do when you can't pay your bills?"

"I'm going to finish the fucking book, Christopher, now shut the fuck up about it."

He reached for a nearby bottle of water and gulped half of it in an angry flash of energy.

Christopher stood in place. "I think what you need is something new to care about."

85

"Yeah, I know what you think…I get it…It's not happening," he said, running out of breath faster with each phrase.

"It doesn't have to be another girl. Something. Anything. A new hobby. Something for you to fixate on. Thinking about her, the drinking – they're blocking the only healthy addiction you have, your work."

He didn't like when Christopher gave the kind of advice he actually needed. "But if it ends, I'll keep on having nothing to do."

"You're not even making sense. Can you stop messing around?"

He'd lain flat on the floor and whirled the bottle like a baton. "I know…what you're trying to do…and I know…you care…and I thank you for that…"

Christopher interrupted, "And you're gonna say 'but…' and then some clever deflection. Save it."

"I'm just not ready to feel all this. I still don't know what it means. We didn't break up; we took a break…and that got more serious a little at a time…until she stopped speaking to me. What does it even mean?"

"You're the most sentimental asshole on earth. That shit hurt *me*. I know it hurt you."

"Whatever…Sure, yeah…I'm not hiding that I feel awful. I think it's pretty clear. But there's nothing I can do about it. I'm not ready to address it."

"I'm just trying to make sure you don't die before you can," Christopher said.

"I'm not going to die. I'm never going to die."

"Yeah. I know."

"Thanks, boy."

The door pounded again. "Uh, Christopher...Joey apparently invited these girls over, they're in the living room –"

Christopher rolled his eyes. "Jesus Christ."

"Go throw them out of the club."

"Yeah. Try to stay up a bit longer," Christopher said, then raced from the room to avert certain neutering by Cody's betrothed.

The door closed and he blacked out with the light.

Coffee Again

He tapped the "End" button on his phone hard, relishing that Christopher couldn't hear him slamming it down in frustration. There wasn't much more "I told ya so" he could take – not least because he hated admitting the dog was right. A few more days of fluids, he thought, and he'd feel like himself. He slunk to his bedroom to retrieve a new set of black clothes and his old, green flannel (the one that made him feel like his street was the set of his very own Screaming Trees music video), worn to its last few threads by the events that preceded many another "I told ya so." Rejuvenated by the scent of the shirt, he powered out the door, down the dreary cement stairs, and out into the thin, fall air. He paused for a moment to enjoy it; he hated the summer's humid smell. He pressed on to the café.

Another mid-afternoon quest for freedom intercepted by a long series of picky, dozen-ingredient smoothies. Each took their typical two minutes to mix and serve. He felt terrible for James and Candy behind the counter who, somehow, seemed never to expect the 3 PM rush. And why should they? Surely, nobody with a traditional job should be about it in the middle of the afternoon. But the mixed scent of coffee beans and tea leaves – and the conditioning to anticipate the first long, cool gulp of his tea – began to wake him from the last trails of sleep, and he turned from the counter and began to search the row of two-top tables along the windowsill for something unoccupied, and then, there she was again. Her hair concealed each side of her face and what remained visible was obscured by a familiar, thick textbook.

The same curious feeling he'd had after their first encounter overtook him. He wasn't excited to see her. He wasn't nervous either. He was relieved.

"Well, say something… Please..." he begged.

"Hmm?" She glazed over one of his scratched-up notebooks, one hand holding it, the other rested on her cheek, her hair falling over half her face.

"I'm dying here."

"Hmm…Wow." The excitement in her voice didn't match her flat expression.

"What?"

She closed the book and slid it across the table. "Well, it's wonderful."

"Are you sure?"

"Yes, it's very sweet, sad, honest, the words are nice."

"But does it do anything?" he asked, eyes dodging from the book to her and back.

Quietly, she searched the ceiling and walls. "Ah, that question."

"Mmm." He wouldn't look away.

"Yes, it does a lot. It pulls someone into their own regret, maybe... Makes them long for an old flame."

"What does it do for you?"

"Well..."

He qualified before she could answer, "And not the same pull. Not what you know it'll do to other people. Just you."

She seemed unwilling to answer in seriousness until she did. "Well, I don't know if I've had any flames this blue before. So, for me, it just makes me feel for you— err, uh, the speaker."

"Heh, you can say 'me,' that's alright. Don't think I'm fooling anyone." *Certainly not you.*

She laughed. "Well... *you* are, clearly, still very much in love with her."

He slouched. "New words, old wounds."

"If you say so."

"Why don't you believe me?" he asked, unsure where the vulnerable feeling sprouted from.

She laughed again. "You're very direct."

"Never got anywhere by tiptoeing."

"But it's graceful to tiptoe." There was a punitive niche to each of her corrections.

"Well, sure," he course-corrected, "It's my favorite way to travel."

"But you never get anywhere?" she smirked.

"Never."

90

"But it's your favorite way?" She kept her eyes in a fixed, critical direction while she straightened her posture.

"Definitely." He sat up, too.

"Heh, you're hopeless."

"Nearly." *You don't know the half of it.*

She sipped on her coffee. "Hmm."

"So, why don't you believe me?"

"I just don't believe that anybody could write something so sad and longing about someone they don't love."

"That's as much a challenge as a compliment, huh?" he wondered aloud.

"Much more a challenge."

"Well, let me say it this way: when the last of it ended, I couldn't have written it. That's for sure. I mean, I couldn't breathe. For weeks it was just sleeping and eating. The usual story. Whatever this is," he held the notebook up, "it wasn't happening."

"If you say so."

"Truly." *She won't believe a word I say.*

"So, now that it's over, you're living in it constantly so you can write about it?"

He laughed. "Well, I'm nothing if not an accomplished masochist."

Disarmed for an almost imperceptible second, she mocked, "I'll keep that in mind —"

"Oh, no, don't!" he yelped.

"Hahaha! Too late."

"Ugh."

"But alright, I believe you." She nodded in disbelief.

"Hey, good then." Sipping his tea, he listened to the rhythm she tapped on the table with her fingertips. It was chipper. Perhaps she wasn't as anxious to move onto other conversation as he feared.

"So, do you always write this sad?" she said, a hint of joy in the accusation.

"Only when I'm that sad."

"So?"

"Yeah, most of the time."

"Heh." She slouched.

"You want another coffee?"

She perked up, then said too casually, "Uh, sure."

"Okay, be right back."

"Okay."

He stood up from the high-top table and adjusted his jeans and his collar. There were only two people in line ahead of him.

"Same thing?" he called to her from line.

"Yeah, thank you!" she called back. He had, more or less, known that. But it was a nice excuse to look at her body language from across the café. It seemed as if the moment he'd stood up, she'd buried herself back in her book. He liked that. The first guest approached the counter and ordered a strange, iced coffee blend he didn't recognize – it was about fifty degrees outside, so, he thought to himself, *you can spot a coffee junkie at least twelve feet away*.

He turned to review the way she sat and read. She crossed her left leg over her right and leaned over them to the table. She had the book upright, held it by one hand, and glided the other down the ends of the unturned pages. She seemed every bit uninterested in him, only in the book.

He planted the next round on the table between them. "Hey, here ya go."

"Thank you so much, here's the cash—" she reached across, a few singles already rolled in her fist.

"Don't worry about it. I've got this insane-person unlimited card."

"I see. A bad habit, huh?"

"Not really. Got enough of those as it is. Just a gift." He sank down into the seat.

"Ah, thank goodness – I was almost afraid you weren't very well adjusted or something."

"Hahaha. Nice."

Impressively, she gulped the hot mixture right away, then returned it to the table with a demonstrative slam. "So, what're you working on today?"

"More of the non-working on my book, sadly."

She raised her glass and deepened her voice, "It's a terrible burden that you're courageous to bear."

"At least...*someone* understands my suffering..." he said, feigning exasperation. They laughed. "What about you?"

"Notes for a term paper about Chaucer," she ran her hands over the back cover of another textbook, sneaking halfway out of her bag.

"Ah, that's fun." Unsure whether she'd find it cooler if he was serious or in jest, he said it flatly." They making you read the Middle English?"

"Actually, no, but I would have loved that."

A trembling laugh leaked from him. "And you said *I* wasn't well adjusted."

"Ha. Seriously. I love language and that would have been so much fun. I'd prefer translating to deciphering the meaning. The meaning isn't objective."

"Neither is the translating," he said, "If you want to nitpick a bit."

She sighed. "True. But still, I prefer it. Besides, it couldn't be a newer story? In a thousand years, do you think I'll somehow be the first person to have some theory about *The Canterbury Tales*? Why couldn't I be the first person to have a theory about something new? That'd be fun."

He contained a full-of-himself, affirming grin best he could. "It would. Soon, I'm sure."

Her phone vibrated on the table. She picked it up. "Hi, oh, my goodness, I'm sorry, I completely forgot. I'll be there as soon as I can. Okay. Yes. Bye." Frantically, she gathered her things from the table and filled her bag.

"Everything okay?" he asked.

"Yeah, I'm just late for a family thing. I'm sorry. It was great to talk to you again!"

"Definitely," he said, as time slowed down. He had to decide. Christopher would probably kill him, legitimately, if he didn't ask for her name. But, to himself, asking for her name was choosing that he had interest in her. He knew that he didn't. He had made a choice, and he should stick by it for his own honor. How could he prove to himself that he wasn't doing what Christopher thought he should do in the first place if he made the effort?

"Hey, wait," he fumbled out. Time regained its speed. "Sorry, I just realized that I never even caught your name."

"Oh, I'm sorry. That's crazy. How did we just...for hours and never...? Never mind. I'm Lily."

"Hi, Lily."

"And here," she ripped a scrap of paper from a notebook and scribbled on it. "Call me sometime. We should hang out."

He smiled at her and read the scrap.

"See ya later."

When he looked up, she had gone.

Suspiciously easy, he thought. If she suspected interest in either direction she'd not have given her number so easily. He was in the clear. He had made a new friend.

It is, perhaps, the most monumental biological setback that mankind has yet to evolve beyond – that most people cannot imagine a relationship with someone of the opposite sex without thinking about the sex. That is, it's ridiculous that many people can't, but even worse is that many more assume this is true of everyone else. Shouldn't it be biologically serving to have allies in every tribe, everywhere, of every sort? Shouldn't it be common for a man to be friendly with a woman without once considering whether she is a viable partner?

Is there something unsettling about this qualm? Is the only reason someone might consider it that they have become so emotionally and physically repressed by confusion or bitterness that they cannot bring themselves to find anyone attractive? Or is there some deeper realization they might have when growing past those carnal assumptions?

Perhaps a friendship between a man and a woman can reach depths of reflection and respect unknown to same-sex friendships because of this; perhaps there're things to be learned and shared – like settlers encountering natives in a new colony. Who knows?

JUNK, he wrote over it.

Post-Nuptials

"So, you're telling me—" Christopher spat. He was exploding through the phone.

"Yes," he deadpanned. Gradually, with a smile, he sank back into his favorite cushion on

the couch and breathed comfortably.

"That you ran into the same girl—"

"Yes." *Oh, goodie – he's really eating it up.*

Angrier with each phrase, Christopher breathed heavy, getting no louder but boiling

over dumbfounded. "In the same place—"

"Yes."

"At the same time—"

"Yes."

"And had an even better conversation—"

"Yep."

With a burst, the grinding friction of his vocal cords showing, Christopher yelled, "And

you *didn't get her fucking phone number?*"

Finally, he laughed aloud. "Relax, old boy, I'm fucking with you."

"Jesus. What, do you have a death wish? I mean, I was five seconds from booking a flight to come murder you. I'm on the app on my phone. My finger was on the Confirm button."

He giggled like a child. "I'm sorry. Couldn't help myself. Her name is Lily, I got her number; we had a very nice conversation – and I'm not asking her out."

"Jesus fucking Christ."

"I'm not interested in her."

"Then why did you get her number?" Christopher prodded with a smirk.

"Actually, when I asked her name to be polite, she gave me the number without my asking. So, I didn't." He yawned and set his legs up across the couch.

"Wait, wait, wait. She volunteered her number?"

"Yeah." Another yawn.

Impatiently, Christopher barked, "And you're not asking her out?"

"Nope."

"What in the name of God is wrong with you?"

"Hah. Nothing. She's great, very sweet, nice to talk to. Why should I think anything more than that?" Another yawn, louder – *one of these will really piss him off.*

Christopher might have been foaming at the mouth. "Because she's clearly into you – because she gave you her phone number."

"Christ – you know, not everything is part of the same neurotic social articulation." He took a breath to aim his crosshairs. "Sometimes, adult human beings can rise above the most primitive and unimaginative thoughts they might have had and be friendly to one another."

"What the *fuck* did you just say? What the fuck is wrong with you? Neurotic? What are you talking about?"

"What?"

Christopher erupted. "These are *the rules*. They're not some arbitrary, lighthearted extravagance set in motion by pampered aristocrats to occupy themselves with meaningless minutiae like the bullshit you write. They're the way everyone communicates from here to every tiny island in the Pacific, rich and poor, any color, denomination, sexuality, any time – these are the rules."

"Dear God." With his mouth closed he cackled at Christopher's rage.

"And the rules outline specifically that when someone volunteers their *phone number*, in the way *she* did, she wants him to *call her and ask her out*!"

"Haha. Sure, yes, very funny, great. I don't think the normal rules apply here. I'm not interested in them, and she thinks like I do – so I don't believe she is, either."

Moping, Christopher resigned, "What's happening to you?"

"What?"

"What's happened to my boy? Come back to us! You've turned to the dark side. This is an unmitigated disaster."

"Hahaha."

"It's not funny, dammit!" Christopher almost broke character and laughed himself.

"It's pretty funny – you're deranged!"

"Jesus Christ. You're outrageous. You're stuck in there for months, whining about how sad and drunk you are, how purposeless you feel – and this woman who fills every blank and checks every box just materializes at the coffee shop. And you're not going to ask her out?"

He grinned to himself. "Nope. If I don't see her for a while, I'm going to call her, say 'hello,' and ask if she wants to hang out some time. You're free to live in the prison of your deluded, Woody Allen-George Costanza world. I'm just trying to make friends."

With the airy tone of preparing to say 'alright, I've got to go do something, speak to you later,' Christopher argued lazily, "What're you, five years old? It's nice and everything, really. Your little pipedream about people. Sure, not everyone's an innately sexual being. You're proving that right now, you selfish, stupid bitch."

"Ha."

"But you have no right to fly in the face of the ancient ways – our *traditions* – just to prove a point. A point you will fail to prove by the way."

"How could I fail to prove anything?" Itching to be done with it, he regretted the question right away. "I'm not interested in her, and I'm not asking her out. If she wants to be more than friends, that's too bad – I'm not doing that."

"How *dare* you, you dog! You unsympathetic wretch. There are those of us who would collapse in salvation if a woman who shared all our interests just appeared in our favorite coffee shop and offered us her phone number."

Through more cackles, he almost yelled, "Ah, therein lies the problem for you."

"Of *course* that's the problem for me!"

"Hahaha."

Christopher wound up and attacked. "So, you know what you're going to do, asshole? You're going to call her – not tomorrow, not sometime in the future, maybe, but *now* – and you're going to ask her out to dinner, and phrase it in a way that clearly implies you're asking her on a date. And she's going to say yes, and you're going to go out with her and have a great time. And if you ever, in the rest of our lives, think you're going to threaten me again with this abject nonsense, I swear to God I'm going to kill you."

"Ha! Alright, I'll make a deal with you. I'm not going to ask her out – I'm not interested in dating her. But I will call her now to see if she'd like to get together."

"You're revolting. You're a vile *specimen*."

"And I'm going to be very friendly and make it clear that I'm being friendly," he said.

"I think I'm going to kill you right now," Christopher said. I've hidden a cluster bomb under your sink for exactly this sort of occasion. I was always worried you'd go completely insane. If you don't stop talking crazy right now, I'm going to blow up your apartment."

"Hahaha – Jesus Christ. That's it then. Blow me up. It's been a pleasure."

"Yours is...a tragic loss...but one I'll have to be willing to endure."

"Ha."

"Are we not going to discuss the obvious?" Christopher pivoted without warning.

He guessed at wedding concerns. "That you are dumb for buying a tuxedo?"

"Haha! To the contrary – the number of weddings we're likely confronting over the next five years or so renders me a genius for having bought my tuxedo."

"Let's hope you remain every inch the Christopher you are today, then, for the maintaining of the dignity of that tuxedo," he teased.

"Fuck off."

"Ha!"

After a silence, Christopher mumbled, "Yeah, you're right about that, actually."

"I know. That's why you rent, baby." He had never rented a tuxedo before and didn't know what the fuck he was talking about.

"Fuck," Christopher said, halfway laughing because he didn't mind spending the money, only hated the prospect of shopping again.

"I'm calling her now. I'll let you know what happens."

"Alright, speak to you later."

"Yep."

He laughed imagining Christopher stuffed in the same tuxedo thirty years later, color sapped, seams loosened, really making the buy worth it.

Sat up on the same couch cushion, he waited anxiously as the phone rang. *Too soon. Doesn't matter for a friend. Still kind of weird. Who cares though, right? No potential consequ-*

"Hello?"

"Hi there, Lily?"

"Yeah – hi! How are you?" Her spectrum of chipper was no wider than his, just more easily deployed.

He stuttered at first, "Good, thank you, how are you?"

"I'm good. Just off work."

"Oh, I'm sorry to bother—"

"Oh no, I'm not doing anything. What's up?"

"Well, maybe this is kind of strange, but I thought maybe you'd like to get together and hang out." His stutter wasn't smoothing out much.

The phone was silent for a few wrenching seconds. "You mean like, go on a date?"

"No, actually, I thought we could just get together and, uh, spend time together, talk, have a drink, maybe watch a movie."

"So, not a date?" she asked again.

"No."

"Oh." It sounded neither disappointed nor relieved, just flat.

He fumbled around what to say. "Did you want to go on a date?"

"Oh, no. I just figured you were asking me out." Whether the first bit was a lie, he couldn't tell. Again, she was quick to cover any underlying motives.

Finally comfortable, he said, "Well, to be totally straightforward with you, most of my good friends live far away, and I've been very alone recently, and I thought we really got along great. So, I was just hoping that we could keep getting to know each other."

"Oh. Well, yeah, that would be great. What were you thinking to do?"

"We could take a walk someplace, or go to the beach, or get lunch?"

"Sure, we could do that." It didn't sound like she liked the idea.

He pivoted, "Or we could just watch a movie and order some food." He also pivoted in posture, cracking his back to loosen up.

"That would be great, too," she said, uncharacteristically unforthcoming, maybe to measure his suggestions.

Must be decisive. "Okay, want to do that?"

"Yeah, sure. When?"

"What about Friday?"

"Friday I'm going to a play with some friends," she said.

"Saturday?"

"Saturday I'm going to the zoo, actually," she laughed, maybe worried about making too many excuses. "I'm sorry."

"Sunday?" he offered, voice higher pitched with each new day.

"Do you really have nothing to do all weekend?"

"I don't see my friends and I write all night." *Nothing pathetic about that.*

"Okay, Sunday. What time?"

"Seven?"

"So early?" she groaned.

"Well, I thought maybe you had work or class the next morning."

"Thoughtful of you. Okay, seven."

A casual "Okay."

"Okay, nice talking to you. I've got to start heading home," she said.

"Oh, of course. Thanks. Yeah. Looking forward to it."

"Heh, yeah, me too."

Unsure about anything they'd just said, he gushed a sigh of relief to hang up the phone, stood and walked to the DVD shelf, and unsleeved a documentary about the Hittites that his once impervious attention had yet to outlast twenty minutes of.

Non-Eddie

He limped from the door to the bar with a heavy guitar case in his left hand. Gingerly, with his head facing the stacks of liquor but his eyes daggers at her across the bar, he leaned his case to the rail and slid onto a stool, raising a hand. The bartender motioned with his finger, "Just a second," and filled a shot glass with silver tequila.

He followed the barman's hand from the rail and back, to a thin slice of lime wedged over the side of the glass, to a quizzical exchange of expressions to confirm the presentation, and down to the bar in front of her. She thanked the bartender. She snaked her fore and middle fingers around the glass and raised it to her lips, took the shot, then chewed furiously on the lime, slammed the glass back down on the bar, and continued not looking at him but staring at her phone.

"Can I have a Jameson and ginger?"

Five or six jacketed guys with fade haircuts and knock-off Les Pauls were helping construct a make-shift stage, and there was some meandering and purposeless soft rock foaming from the speakers. The bar was way too small for them. She looked around at the room in every direction but his, then back to her phone. He searched for some means of attracting her attention then gave up, reaching first for a cocktail napkin, then for a pen from his jacket pocket, and started scribbling something down. She wasn't biting.

Some time passed, and someone else took over the speakers, replacing the garbage with David Bowie's "Station to Station," livening up the place. Separately, their heads started bobbing to the rhythm.

A few more minutes of nothing.

Finally, she leaned toward him and offered, "So you're playing tonight?"

"Yeah, I think after these guys." He tried to be coy and collected.

"Cool."

"Are you playing?"

"No, just hanging out."

"That's cool, do you know anyone who's playing?" He grasped at straws.

"My boyfriend, he's playing later."

"Oh, cool," he stuttered, failing to hide his disappointment, "What kind of stuff does he play?"

"He plays, like, acoustic alternative stuff. Kind of like Leonard Cohen, very introspective, smart lyrics. Does a lot of picking."

"Oh, wow, that's kind of like what I do."

"Really?"

"Yeah, but I take Waits over Cohen depending on the day of the week," he said. The discovery that this woman wasn't pursuable seemed to elevate his confidence.

She chuckled sympathetically, "You're funny."

"Thanks." He looked back over the scribbles on his cocktail napkin. "Dave," he called at the bartender, "Can I have another?"

His right boot tapped on the beer-stained parquet floor while his left rested on the middle rung of his stool. "I was worried I was dyin', for a long, long time," he mumbled, eyes closed as he bobbled his head to a melody unfamiliar to the rest of the bar, "I was waiting for the shadows to slink by, I had hoped you'd make an offer to pull me out of darkness – baby, you've got all it takes to try." From the corner of his eye, he examined whether the woman was watching. She was not. He kept tapping.

The first band finished tuning up, and a handful of eager jackets had filed into the small room. A crowd, perhaps. "Hi, we're called Radio Silence," the tepid singer mumbled. "This is called Junk House," and so they began. Thrashing about despite the meager dribble therein. She feigned interest throughout but kept checking her phone. He spun his stool to face the band occasionally, clapping but unable to shake the blank expression of purposelessness that had overtaken his face. Mostly he stared at his cocktail napkin.

Between songs he leaned to her, "That was pretty good, a little Pearl Jam-y," and she replied, "Yeah, just less good," under her breath. They laughed. With a few minutes remaining she leaned to him, "Aren't you going on soon?"

"Not if I can help it," he half-whispered. He looked more comfortable.

"Well, you should go on, you'll be great!"

He blushed, "That's sweet of you, I'm just not feeling great about it tonight."

"Hmm, too bad. My boyfriend always says, even when it's a shit night, just play through it. It cauterizes your skin for more bad shows," she smirked.

"Smart guy," he said. "Where's he; isn't he playing soon, too?

"Not sure. Still waiting for him," she said.

"This is going to be our last song," non-Eddie Vedder announced, "Thank you all so much for coming!" The twelve people in the bar nodded and clapped in acknowledgment.

He slid his empty glass across the bar. "Dave, can I have one more?" He was slouched over the bar, half leaning on it, as far from the "stage" as he could make himself. The bartender poured a heavy dose of whiskey and topped it with a dash of ginger ale, and he sarcastically answered,

"Thanksssss," eager to gulp down the courage.

The band finished and left. He sat up, suddenly attentive, picked up his guitar case from beside him and moved towards the stage – then turned back to retrieve his cocktail napkin. He stuffed it in his pocket.

"Good luck," she commanded as he walked away from the bar.

"Thank you," he said back, "I didn't catch your name…"

The speakers interrupted loudly with Incubus's "Summer Romance," and the MC screamed into the microphone, "Thank you so much, Radio Silence! We'll be back in a few minutes with more music!" She had turned around without answering.

He crept towards the stage and set down his guitar, pulled it from its case and strapped it over his shoulder.

"Good luck, man!" said non-Eddie as they passed one another.

"Hey man, thank you. Great stuff tonight," he said back, a matter of karma, mostly.

The MC helped check the sound, and he tuned and pulled the mic stand to his face. A few more people had filled up the small space. It felt a bit more alive.

The music faded out quickly, and without being announced he began: "Good evening."

"Good evening," the audience responded in kind.

He looked around quickly, mostly keeping his eyes on her. He reached into his pocket and pulled out the cocktail napkin, placing it delicately on a barstool beside him. He read it over. "This is called 'Stowaways.'"

He swam through forty minutes of dramatic and exciting folk-alternative experiments, with little interruption but the occasional joke: "Leonard Cohen often said he wished he knew where the good songs came from, or he'd go there more often. I wish he had known too, it's very lonely," and so on. She laughed at the bar. Nobody had sat down next to her.

"Thank you very much," he said, "This will be my last, it's the latest. This is 'Waiting for Winter.'" A respectable applause ended his set.

He collected his things and, looking back at the bar, where she had turned away, he stepped outside.

Minutes later, another guy got on stage, and played beautiful, folky rock for an hour. She attentively clapped, smiled, and kept her phone in her purse for the whole hour. The audience loudly clapped and cheered throughout. He heard them from through the door and felt shitty.

Afterwards, he stumbled back in, leaned his guitar on the bar and sat down again.

"Can I close out?"

The bartender printed a check and left it in front of him, then walked across the bar and pulled down the silver tequila. He poured another shot and sliced a fresh lime and handed it to her.

"Oh, I didn't know you were still here," she said. "I thought you left after your set."

"Just needed some fresh air."

"I see," she said, wrapping her fingers around the shot glass.

"Did your boyfriend ever show up? Isn't he playing tonight?"

"Oh, he played already. He left to get some air."

"Oh, he was the one before? I'm sorry I missed him."

113

"He was good. You're right, you play a lot like him," she said.

"Well," he raised the last sips of whiskey in his glass, "here's to Leonard Cohen."

"Surely," she said. They drank.

He signed his bill and stood up. "Pleasure to meet you," he said softly and extended his hand.

"So nice to meet you," she laughed along and shook his hand back, "You were really good!"

"Thank you, you're too kind." He let go of her hand and turned towards the door.

Still laughing, she stood up and tapped on his shoulder. "Really, you were so great, I'm so proud of you!"

He began to chuckle and wrapped his arms around her waist, "Thank you sweetheart," still laughing, "This was a great idea. Was I actually any good tonight, though?"

"You were spectacular. 'Keeper' sounded amazing." She kissed him on the cheek, and they started towards the door together.

There was something semi-arousing and semi-mystical, the latter in an un-arousing sort of way, about writing experiences like that, word for word, as if they were fiction. It didn't allow him to relive or to fantasize, per se, but it soothed and coached into a mental space where he was comfortable. He wrote that way often. Fiction, he felt, was only as good as the truth it worked its way around. Sometimes, the truth was right for it.

But Sara was very far away now, and "meeting each other as strangers again" seemed even farther. Every day, a few new words scratched themselves onto paper, aimlessly, he thought, trying to outline and detail the pain of the preceding months and make of it a story that anyone else might care about. It just wouldn't appear. He wrote and wrote – revealing paralyzing dread and bold, private items in the hope that some might connect. It wouldn't connect.

Somehow, some way, she would come back. He knew it. He wouldn't jinx it by telling anyone. He didn't really care how long it took. He wasn't drinking because of that.

Christopher barked a familiar line at him over the phone. "You can't do this."

"Why not?" He stood over the kitchen counter, gulping on a blended smoothie of blueberries and mango chunks, eyes wide open, stomach taut, hair combed, and muscles relaxed.

"Because it's not going to be what you think."

"You don't know that – and why would you say it?"

"Because I'm legitimately concerned that it's not going to be what you think."

"Please, trust me, old boy," he reassured. I know it's not ideal. It's not what I want. But what I want is to be with her, and this is the way I can do that, eventually."

"Did you set rules?" Christopher said.

"No."

"Jesus."

"I know what you're thinking. Don't say it," he warned.

"I'm not going to say it because it doesn't need to be said."

"Good."

"Not good." It was good that Christopher would get pissed for him, surely.

He breathed out. "Okay, right, it's not good, but I had no choice."

"Of course you had a choice," Christopher stammered. "You always have a choice, and you pretend that you don't. I don't know what's happened to you."

"I made a choice, and I'm living by it."

"What happens if this goes as badly as you know it has the chance to?"

"I'll have to hope it doesn't and reassess if it does," he said confidently.

"It's not like you to be so passive about something so important."

"No, it's not. I do what I must."

"You can be with her in the end without having no balls at all," Christopher said.

"How might you have suggested that?"

"You could have done this yourself."

"What?" He gulped down the rest of his smoothie and ran it under the sink.

"You could have suggested this yourself. Then you'd be exactly where you are now, but with your self-respect intact."

"No, I wouldn't. I'd have hurt her, which I wouldn't want to do regardless, and she'd also have less respect for me, which I could never want."

"Your priorities are just her priorities, then."

He gulped meekly. "Well, we both know a few people who think that way."

"We do – and you usually mock them for thinking that way."

Christopher was torching him in all the right places, and he was running out of defense.

"They don't have the same relationship I do."

"I'm sure they think that about themselves."

"I'm sure they don't think about anything at all," he said.

Christopher got quieter and slower. "Ha. That may be true, but I still believe you're making a mistake."

"I know I'm not. We can table this if you like. I'm not changing my mind."

"I know. And I'm sorry. I hope I'm wrong." Solemn Christopher was scarier.

"Yeah."

"I hope it doesn't take too long."

"Yeah."

117

The Cave

"Hey, man, what's up?"

Holding his phone to his ear between a thumb and forefinger, he resisted the temptation to sigh impatiently into the speaker. He'd spent months waiting for the call. His back to the kitchen counter, he poured a count of scotch into the nearest empty glass, its inside sticky-dry from the last. "Hey, Si, how's it going?"

"Just working, you know, nothing special." Simon was at the crossroads of chipper and

nerve-wracked on the other end.

"Yeah, same here," he said.

"What're you working on? Anything new?"

Early deflection. Nobody actually calls just to say, 'what's up?' This is big. "Yeah,

the usual. Got a bit done, a lot more to go."

Simon cooled off a bit. "I definitely hear that, man. I'm working on this new record – the band totally sucks, but they think they're amazing. They won't use a click track because their drummer insists he keeps perfect time – he's always off. Singer has 'perfect pitch,' so he won't use the computer – always pitchy."

"That's terrible man, I'm sorry about that." He sipped half what he'd poured and exhaled

the sting, waiting for the real conversation to begin.

"It's okay, just frustrating."

"Yeah."

Simon gulped himself and stayed quiet a moment. "So, the reason I'm calling, man, is because I'm going to ask Penny to marry me."

"Really?" he asked, summoning as much earnest surprise as he could.

"Yeah."

"That's great news, man; that's awesome. How long have you been thinking about it?"

"In general? For years," Simon said, very happy with himself.

"No, I mean, recently – when did you decide?"

"I guess the last few weeks, really. You know, with Cody's coming up, I just decided it was time."

He sneered, a performance for himself. "That's great, Si. I'm so happy for

you."

"Thank you, bud. Thanks so much."

"Let's just hope she says yes then, huh?" he ribbed, polishing the drink after.

"Haha. Yeah. Well, I think she will," Simon said, the confidence a little gross, if well founded. "I mean, she's wanted me to ask her for a while now."

"She definitely has."

"What?"

"Well," he course-corrected, "She's clearly wanted to get married for a while. At least, that's what the group seems to think."

"Really?" There was some real shock underneath Simon's question, a telegraph that he

hardly picked up on anything their mutual friends ever discussed.

That was probably to his friend's better health, he thought. "Well, yeah."

"Oh."

"Did you speak to Christopher about this?" "Right before you," Simon said.

"Good. What did he say?"

"He congratulated me, said he'd help out, and that was it."

"Okay, great," he said, his dominant hand, free of the phone, practicing the motions to

click End Call and dial Christopher.

"Yeah."

"It's going to be wonderful, Si. I can't wait. You know I love Pen. I couldn't be happier for you guys."

"Thanks. It is going to be great. Thank you."

"Of course."

Simon sighed his relief. "Well, if you'll excuse me – I just have to call my folks and stuff. Get everyone's opinions."

"Of course. Go ahead. I'll speak to you soon. Lots to talk about, I guess," he said with a chuckle.

"Yeah. And hey, man, I just wanted to say, I know it's been hard for you recently. I'm really sorry. I'm here for you, if you want to visit, if you want us to come down there, anything you need – you're not alone, okay?"

"Thanks, Si. I'm okay. Don't worry."

"Okay. Talk to you soon."

"Yeah." Reaching over the counter and the faucet, he carefully placed the glass under the sink and ran the water until it was filled. He dialed Christopher with the other hand.

"You get the call?" Christopher answered.

"I did."

"Can't believe this shit."

"I mean…I can," he snickered.

"Ha. Well, yeah."

"The second we heard from Penny, we should have figured she was already telling his family and everyone else to talk to him."

"Yep."

Fingers making rounds over his chin, he kept speculating. "It's good, though. It was always going to happen; now there will just be a date on it."

Christopher interrupted, "Speaking of *dates*, you ungrateful sidewinder—"

"Haha…"

"So, did you call?"

"Yes, I did."

121

"And? What happened?" Right back under the interrogation chair he went.

"It was so fucking awkward."

"Why? I thought you said the conversation with this girl was great."

"It was, but as soon as I asked her to hang out, she asked if it was 'like a date.'"

Christopher finished for him, "And when you said no, it became awkward."

"Yeah."

"I *told* you. I'll take my money now," Christopher taunted.

"We didn't wager on that, actually – but you're also not right." He stammered, "It was awkward, and maybe she had been hoping it was a date – but that doesn't mean she won't be fine with us being friends."

"That's not what our debate was about. I told you it wouldn't be as advertised. Either she would be pissed, or you would get hurt. She's clearly pissed now, whatever comes of it all later."

He objected, "That doesn't count, and you know it. She's not shallow, and I'm not looking for anything else. That's it."

"We will see. In the meantime, when are you seeing her?" Christopher ignored.

"Sunday night."

"Jesus."

"We're just hanging out– time to put your compass and calculator away."

Christopher laughed. "Where?"

"My place."

"You invited her to your apartment to hang out as friends?"

"That's what friends do, isn't it?" *Coyness will kill him.*

"What the fuck is wrong with you?"

"Nothing, can you quit it?"

Christopher could never quit it. "She's coming over to your apartment on a Sunday night, the first time you've ever seen her outside of the coffee shop, and you're just going to watch a movie and talk?"

"That's what you and I would do."

"She's not me."

"Evidently."

"This is all sorts of weird and uncool."

"Do you have female friends?" he asked.

"Besides Alyssa and Penny, no."

"Exactly. I like having female friends. You're being ridiculous. This is that simple."

"It's not – you're lying to yourself and to me. I can't tell which is worse, but both deserve punishment. Thankfully for me and for justice, you will be punished immensely when you come to the realization that you do have feelings for her, and she doesn't for you because of this nonsense, or the realization that she has feelings for you and won't settle for being your friend. Either way, you'll have to choose what to do." By the end, Christopher was very satisfied.

"It's not a choice," he said. I've only got eyes for Sara, and I'm very clear about it."

"Are you?"

"Why are you trying to convince me otherwise?"

"I told you before. I think you need a new thing to obsess about and take seriously. I think you need to screw your head on straight and learn how to care about anything other than Sara again."

"Well, I do care about other things. Why don't you ask Cody if anything is more important than Alyssa?" A smug, unworthy answer, perhaps – but Christopher deserved it.

"They're engaged."

"Same kind of relationship."

"No, it's not. However much one person loves another, once they're married, they've locked in and committed. You know that. It's not the same. You're lying and you're a trash can," Christopher said.

"I'm not. This is all much simpler than you're pretending."

"You always wanted to avoid becoming a cliché more than anything else…This really is a pity."

"Have you heard from the massage therapist?" he said fast.

Christopher played up the awkward reply. "Well, no, but, uh…Why don't we just forget about that for the moment."

"You know what? You can do whatever you want."

"Ha. The Great Cliché, boy – think about it."

"Okay. Thanks very much. I'm going to have a drink and try to write something. Speak to you later."

"Good luck, boy…"

A little pissed, he hung up and set the phone down hard. He reviewed old notes and paragraphs. Some of the ideas were interesting; most were pathetic. He ripped a few up, then poured himself a scotch and drank it, fast. Like he was hit by lightning, he fell down in the couch and slept.

It was a familiar dream. He saw himself in the third person, sitting on a park bench someplace near home. His childhood home, not here. There was a path, a series of hills, and a long, winding lake in front of him. Nobody was around but ducks and bugs.

> He leaned forward on the rusty metal bench and stared into the distance, taking in the park and the lake – but mostly in the effort to see himself as he imagined he was: utterly hopeless, dramatic, hijacked by mourning and regret, and very cool. It never struck him that nobody could ever be brought to imagine him in the same way. Considering his options for being saved, he gripped the neck of a bottle through a crumpled paper bag and thought to himself, surely, despite everything, he had learned something over these years. There was suddenly no grand, mythological adventure to which he was the Morning and Evening Star. No eternal resuscitation from the crippling woeful expression that had crept across his face. No hidden optimism, cloaked beneath his fabricated shroud of misery – the crack from which the light snuck in. All that was gone.

And in the void remained the hollow shadow of a deeper one. He stared across the park that appeared empty of birds tweeting or squirrels rushing about, of people on their morning run or strolling their newborns, and in the distance, he watched himself crawling into a black cave, quite content to make no progress through it, quite unimpressed by any light at the end of it, quite uninspired to dig. And sitting on the wet, muddy floor of the cave, his hands tensing up in the damp cold and his shoulders shivering and his blood cooling in the dim, it was quiet. Every grasp he'd tightened around a jewel had clenched it through his fingers, but it was quiet. Every word he'd exfoliated from his skin had toughened it just enough that he could survive the next beating, but never fight back – quiet.

And the cave would echo that quiet, and he'd hear ideas repeating themselves to him about the way he could go beyond, the ways he could get even, the ways he could recover and find a semblance of happiness, but he deafened his ears to them and enjoyed his fantasy. The cave was for suffering; it was for him to be alone. It was magnificent – he had never been so thoroughly hopeless. So many thoughts, words, jewels would be drawn from his poor brain down there. In the cold and damp, he actually began to believe all that, and some words started to form in his head about years languished and dreams forfeited, and he remembered that everything he'd ever done was to suffer now and write these words down. He was just then getting there.

He brought the bottle to his mouth and gulped down more of the cave.

He didn't remember rising from the couch to put it all down. *Alright,* he marked between sips.

The Midtown East

She'd never wear jeans, and she'd never wear sneakers. She'd try any style of cigarette, but something grievously offensive evidenced itself in jeans and sneakers. How could I possibly love this woman, he thought, who despises my favorite things so easily? A few Septembers later he couldn't remember how he'd ever given a shit about jeans and sneakers.

A pile of clothes had accumulated on the foot of her bed. He sat beside them watching her try on one sweater after another. They smiled at one another when they locked eyes in the mirror over her dresser.

"Oh my God," she scowled at herself, "This sweater makes me look terrible."

He grabbed her nearest hand and reassured, "Nothing could do that."

She smiled, then let it become a scowl as she ripped off the knitted fabric and threw it onto the pile, "No, it's horrible. I want to get rid of all my clothes and start again."

"You know, I think that's a great idea. You're sick of all this stuff. It'll be fun."

"Wanna come shopping with me?" she offered.

"Of course I do. Especially if I can watch you try everything on."

She rolled her eyes and smiled again, pulling more sweaters from drawers and tossing them before trying them on.

"Don't worry – we're going to find plenty of things," he pleaded.

After a few moments and a warm glance to him, she said back, "Sorry I'm a crazy person," fishing.

"You just know what you like. You'd be crazy not to complain when you're upset."

"When did you get so nice?"

"I just love you," he answered as she sat down on the bed across from him. "Makes it easy to be nice all the time."

She smiled and picked up her phone, searching for something.

He just kept staring at her, stretching his arms out, massaging her shoulders, scanning the room for details he might want to remember later. He didn't mind when she disappeared into her phone – he needed time to himself, briefly.

"Mall is open until 9:30," she resumed, "Can we go in a few minutes?"

"Sure, of course," he mumbled back, already tired. "Are you hungry?"

She glared at him menacingly, "I'm always hungry, rube!"

They laughed back and forth.

"Where do you feel like going?"

"Hmm," they each wondered aloud.

She hated when they were indecisive – when he was indecisive – and he felt pressure building to choose a place.

"I'll go wherever you want," she said.

"I could do Japanese, I could do Italian, anything. Do you feel like anything in particular?"

"No, I'll go wherever you want."

"Sushi?" he proposed with a smirk – her recent favorite.

"Yeah…"

"Great, I'm in the mood for that. Ha, I'm always in the mood."

"Me too," she said. "Can you start the car and I'll meet you outside?"

"Surely." He hopped up from the bed, never letting go of her hand, rubbed her cheek against it, and walked out to his car. He thought, in just an hour or two, she'd have a whole new selection of leggings, sweaters, and sunglasses that are only narrowly distinguishable from those strewn across her bedroom – but these will have a magical power of fulfillment. If only, he thought, he could soothe his trepidations in the same way, with a new pair of jeans or sneakers. But he already had a few of each. Why buy more?

The phone rang from the floor next to the coffee table. Groggily, he leaned off the couch with one side, reaching with as little energy as possible, and, eventually, was able to squeeze the sides of the phone with his thumb and middle finger and pull it up to his eyes. "Christopher," it read.

"Yes, what is it? What do you want?" he said with no gaps of air between each word.

"Well, hello, boy."

"What are you up to this…morning."

"Hmm," Christopher half-laughed through his breath. "It's six PM."

"Alright."

"Nothing in particular. You?"

"Nothing, if I have anything to say about it."

"Heh. How are you holding up?"

"Not."

"Well, that's for the best. Wouldn't want you moving on or getting over before you finish the book.," Christopher said, concealing, poorly, the real tone and effort of his call.

"Quite right. Well, if that'll be all…" he baited.

"Nah-ah. I'm afraid there's real news from the front today."

"Fuck. What?"

"Cody and Alyssa…"

He shook his head awake. "No way."

"What?"

"They broke up?"

"No. What? No." Christopher cleared his throat.

"Oh. What happened?"

"They've postponed until April."

"Oh. Well, alright. Whatever," he slouched back down.

"Don't you see what's happening here?" Christopher's frantic irony was great fun.

"What?"

"*You* did this. You said the tuxedo wasn't going to be good for me for very long – you *summoned* the delay with your evil voodoo counter-curse!"

"Hahaha! Yeah, and, you know what? I think a delay to their arbitrary, placeholding ceremony that only fills in documentation for the lifestyle they already have was a worthwhile sacrifice to confirm my spellcasting. Now, you shan't continue to deny my powers." He heightened the frequency of his voice to parody Christopher's usual tone of self-assurance.

"You're right. This is terrifying."

"Haha. Oh, well. Should we, like, tell them we're sorry?"

"No, who cares?" Christopher said.

"Ha!"

"But, yeah, no – it's not a big deal. I'm sure he'll confirm the new date with you. Something about the catering service."

"Alright, whatever."

"What-*ever*."

"You know what I was thinking about?" he asked.

"Besides exaggerating how sad women are making you in the hope it will make your writing better?" Christopher said.

"Yeah."

"No, besides that, I can't imagine you've been thinking about anything."

He laughed at the prepared bit. "Very good."

"Thank you."

"So, I've been thinking: you ever notice the difference between songs about specific women or experiences versus… songs that are just 'about love?'"

"Like what?"

"Well, for instance, when Leonard Cohen writes about a woman he really loves and misses, the result is '*I'm Your Man*.'"

"Legendary words."

"Legendary words."

"Yes."

He continued, "And when he's just identifying love, he offers us, '*Ain't No Cure for Love*.'"

"Ahaha. Now I understand. Yeah, that's interesting, actually," Christopher said.

"Well, I'm grateful that you expected it not to be."

"Ha."

"He was actually wrong about his greatest work, though," he said, hoping Christopher would already know which tune he referred to.

"What?"

"*Tower of Song* is actually wrong."

"How?" Christopher kept on.

Good — he knew which one I meant. "Well, its central tenet is wrong."

"What's its central tenet?"

With a deep breath he sat up and charged up. "It's about…you know…he's a guy who's been in love many times and each time it's nearly killed him, and he's only survived by writing about it in different forms and planting himself in this eternal, creepy old hotel for the writers who loved too hard for their own good. So now they just care about the writing, and it's constantly tragic, but it never kills them."

"Right."

"But that's a bit wishful, I think."

"How do you mean?" Christopher repeated.

"They actually *encourage* women to kill you in the tower of song."

"Haha. Go on."

"Can you think of some place where your miserable losses of romance might more constantly assault your will to live than the Tower of Song?" he asked.

"I don't know."

"The answer – take it from someone who's not quite a resident, but has had an extended stay – is no."

"Hahaha." Christopher thought and challenged him. "But how does that make it wrong?"

"Well, even if they don't just let women waltz around killing men in the Tower, all its residents are spending every waking hour thinking of all the ways women have already nearly killed them – without that, you can't get admitted."

"Right, so, if you're doing the kind of work you're expected to in the Tower of Song, the woman you're writing about will sneak through the work and kill you more easily," Christopher pieced together, not without irritated strain leaking into his voice.

"More or less."

"Sounds like less."

He admitted, "Definitely less."

"Well, it's still as good a way to die as any."

"You'd reconsider that if you knew."

"Oh, I think I know," Christopher insisted with yearning in his voice.

"Do you really think you know?"

"Well, just think about right now. Three women, no calls, no hope – I think I gain entry."

He beat back. "But how much do you care about any of them in particular? I don't know if you're feeling the kind of slow death that's usually required."

"Oh, so you're the one deciding?"

"No," he chuckled, "But if I'm going to put my name on the line to recommend you to the committee, I need to know that you really love one of these women and that their unwillingness to return that love is actually going to kill you."

"Hmm. I'll have to think on that."

"Good idea."

"What got you in?" Doubt preceded the question.

"I had a ring picked out for that last one."

"Oh."

Ah, I had forgotten to tell him. "Yep."

"I see."

"Yeah." Matter-of-fact was the only way to dispense that information so late.

"Not, uh, not good."

"Well, it might have been," he corrected.

"Oh, it might have been grand."

"Yeah."

"Why didn't you ever tell me about that?" Christopher said after a while.

"Well, you would have told me I was an idiot."

"No!" Christopher dramatized, "I'd have *never*!"

"Ha! And then I'd have said, 'But I love her, so I've got to.'"

"And then…"

He finished for them both, "And then the year would have proceeded as it has."

"Not good."

"Not." A smirk crept across his face in silence as he considered the hole he'd dug since.

Christopher broke the silence. "So, what would you propose in place of the Tower of Song?"

"Now *that's* interesting."

"Should I give you some time for that one?"

"No, let me see here…a more honest version would be an objective or a clue rather than a place…" he trailed off in desperate, unfocused thought.

"Sounds like you need some time for that one," Christopher teased.

"No, wait…" he begged.

After a minute or two of a silent phone speaker, Christopher barked, "Waiting."

"Okay, got it. This is the Allegory of the Midtown East."

"The Midtown East?"

"The Midtown East." Once his favorite hotel, it made a familiar and clear setting for a Socratic warning.

"Okay."

He began, "Once there was a young man who was very interested in a woman."

"Okay," Christopher answered with a laugh.

"And he expressed his interest, and she returned it – but he was about to move from New York to California. They agreed to keep in touch and see where things went, and after a few more months of talking, they found themselves so enamored with each other that they proclaimed themselves a couple from afar."

"I'm noticing something familiar here."

He proceeded without acknowledging. "So, these months went by, and they were in a dream of bliss, just imagining how wonderful it would be to finally be together – and suddenly he started hearing some bizarre rumors that she was talking the same way with some other guy."

"I see," Christopher said.

"You've heard these stories, yeah? So, our guy thinks to himself, *I don't know what to believe here, but I can't accuse her of doing anything wrong based on a rumor.*"

"Naturally."

"So, this guy goes on talking to this woman for a while longer, but with these rumors swirling around in his head, he starts noticing she doesn't have much time to talk anymore, she's saying stuff that's kind of suspicious, and here and there he convinces himself the rumors were true – so he starts talking to other people, too," he said.

"Ah."

"Totally distraught and unwound, he waits a few days until he can't take it anymore – her lingering distance and inconsistent talking helped convinced him she was guilty – and he tells her they shouldn't go on as they have. So, they go their separate ways."

"This isn't much of an allegory, boy," Christopher interrupted.

He wasn't slowed. "*So*, a few months passed, and our guy becomes increasingly depressed and lonely, and he suspects he's made a huge mistake. He's felt no romantic connection to anybody else in that time, and he knows only one thing could really give him more hope. So, he calls the girl."

"Bold."

"And, somehow, she answers. He apologizes for leaving but doesn't have the heart to tell her why he did – so he tells her about how depressed he was, and difficulties being so far away, and begs her to give him another chance. She doesn't – not right away. But the door is reopened, and they speak for a few weeks, and they swing back into their rhythm, and they start up again."

"Yes. I have heard these stories before."

"Until, some months later, the rumors start up again, too."

Christopher picked up for him. "And things proceed much in the same way; only this time, he's more distraught to hear of goings-on back home, because he's fallen much farther for the girl since."

"Right," he said. "So, they separate again – but with less clarity, and, unsurprisingly, the pattern repeats itself several times. And, finally, after many long years, he returns to New York, and they get steady. And he takes her for their next anniversary, in the toil of summer, for dinner and a show, and they stay at the Midtown East."

"Ah, there it is," Christopher said, his voice as presently exacerbated as he could get it.

"And they have a spectacular night – until, upon returning to the hotel, when they begin to embrace and pull off their show clothes and slink towards the bed. An empty look creeps across her face and her hands run cold and she looks away from him and can't bring herself to look back. She says 'sorry' in a low, hushed voice again and again, slipping under the covers facing the window and lying there, defiantly awake, waiting for him to sleep." He said it all very slowly.

"Jeez."

"He can't take it. He hates to see her so mysteriously affected. He walks around the bed and kneels beside her, looking over her but never forcing eye contact on her. 'What?' she says. 'I'm sorry, sweetheart, I can't take seeing you like this. Won't you tell me what's bothering you?' And, after an hour of silent dread, she sits up and recounts how awfully mistreated she had been by someone else during their most recent time apart. It's a measure irreconcilable, and neither of them can handle it."

"That's awful," Christopher said.

"The pain settles very late, and they fall into a meager sleep that heals nothing."

"So, what's the moral?"

"Not done yet."

"Oh…" Christopher sighed.

"Getting there. So, after a few more months, he decides to correct that near-wonderful weekend, and he invites her back to the city for another dinner, another show, and another shot at the Midtown East. She excitedly accepts – and they go about things much the same way. A beautiful dinner, a thoroughly enjoyable show...and a silent retreat into the reflection of earlier pain when they return to the hotel. This time, though, as if to make up for the years of strangeness, she interrupts her own melancholy, shifts suddenly into a radiant and unstoppable mood, and throws herself at him – but, after a moment, he can sense the dishonest deflection in her feral attack and he holds her, stopping her. They talk about her pain for the rest of the night. A great Christmas."

"Wow."

"And this process, much like the process of their breakups, repeats itself for the following few Christmases, and anniversaries, and Valentines – each time, he slides deeper into the sentiment that all the bad things between them are his fault. If only he had had the courage to ask her whether she was seeing anybody else, years ago, she could have said 'no,' and the rest would have been daisies. Now they both suffer for his cowardice."

"That's bullshit," Christopher interrupted.

"Perhaps," he said. "But it's the truth he lives in. So, they return to the Midtown East for Valentine's Day, and again in rotation. Here and there they have some fun, but, mostly, these near-trysts reveal an outpouring of terror that keeps them up quietly each night. Their daily lives seem totally unaffected by this; it's only a vacation slide."

"That's bizarre."

"And, again and again, it slides. He never stops offering it: 'One day, one Valentine, one Christmas, we'll have the most miraculous weekend together, and it will help fix all of the pain,' he thinks."

"And did it?" Christopher asked ironically.

"Never got the chance. Eventually, she grows tired of the complacency and frozenness that he'd used to survive those years, confusing it for his real person, and she returns to a rotation of leaving him for new and recycled reasons. And he always obliged."

"Awful," Christopher said somberly.

"You see, for our guy, he had never fulfilled the promise and the wish that he'd set out for all those years earlier when they first met. He just wanted to be with this woman in a normal, healthy way. He couldn't see that it wasn't happening no matter how hard he forced it to conform. He was deeply unfulfilled and unhappy, drawing purpose and objective out of her instead of himself. She figured that out first. That's why she kept leaving."

"And the Midtown East?" Christopher asked.

"An innocent bystander. A Ground Zero for the first realization."

"What was that?"

"It was never going to be what he thought," he explained. "Every time he took her to the Midtown East, they were getting farther from starting over."

Christopher laughed at the meager revelation. "You're talking like a man who's dying but you're sounding like a man between rooms in the Midtown East. Or the Tower of Song."

"Heh. Surely I'm a man dying while he waits for one of two doors to appear ajar."

"Surely."

He stared blankly at the blinds, the sun just fallen, no light creeping through the cracks.

Crescendos

It's a slow and plodding series of crescendos, this love industry. You wait hours for a night, or weeks for a year, in each moment the slippery curse of a new instrument of torture slithering its phrases into your ears, mostly on your knees, begging to have the heat of your own melody returned.

Occasionally, it is returned, and when it is, it's much too deafening and satisfying to be likened to the opiates to which it is often compared. When it is, there's the chanting rhythm of sex and a solitary snakeskin of whistled air passed through deep red lips and every note of your wont and sin stepped on deeply as she walks over you. When it is, the chords pass only once in a while. One plea at a time you might send, one instrument offering requests for mercy, another for understanding, another for touch, and you might keep imagining new instruments to deliver the notes of your begging and, in time, have constructed a monument of amorous display, an orchestra of the deepest allure – and you've just got to remind yourself while you're concocting this symphony of humble worship that whatever she's done and whoever she's become in the meantime is alright.

You've just got to want whatever she's willing to return. Otherwise, you might finally start to feel the crescendo building, get her to flood those words back into your ears and glide her body across yours like the harmonies between the woodwinds and strings convinced her to, and only then second guess yourself.

Surely, you'll say to yourself, she could have fashioned some kinder, sweeter, gentler path to this reconciliation than escaping to reconstruct herself, time and again. And you'd better believe you'd be thinking this while those unstoppable, insatiable demands replace the frame of notes that'd grown in their place, filling your head and your body and every player in the symphony with their tune and your choice in the matter would be forfeit. Yeah, when that melody's returned it's all over.

You're not an addict; you're a member of the proletariat. You're scraping together some hard-toiled cash for a train ticket, and you're finding your way to the village to answer the monarch's call to arms. If you've paid your taxes, a few months of waiting patiently and without judgment, you might even get laid. And the most charming part will be how you didn't even care about getting laid. But if it means you're one night closer to holding her hand in public again, you're game. So, you'll be sitting on the edge of her bed, taking the first deep breaths you've taken since before the leaves rolled in, and you'll ask her, gently and smoothly, "Please, can I hear some of that song?" And she won't find it charming at all – she'll get angry, "Didn't I just give you everything?"

She'll be right. You'll have built up layer upon layer of harmony until a cacophony of fierce cries for mercy morphed into a hundred-tone chorus that in its layers conjured her kind of beauty and brought her back into your arms with no right to claim some other justice or balance to any of it. And you'll relent and thank her silently for all you've gotten back and lay beside her, awake for the rest of the night wondering about its audience since then…and convincing yourself how that was all fine. You still won't sleep, though.

It had been long enough without a callback for Christopher's would-be second date. Slumped in his bed in the middle of the afternoon, he'd picked up while still groggy and immediately regretted not staying asleep.

"So, you're telling me I should absolutely *not* text her now?" Christopher's impatient scowl was somehow audible over the phone.

"Not now, not today. Not for a few more days, at least."

"Why?"

"Because you don't have anything to say to her in particular and clearly just want to flirt and try to start something," he said.

"Heh. Yeah. But why shouldn't I do that?" Christopher asked, not as rhetorically as he wished to sound.

"Well."

"Don't you always say girls like it when you're straight up with them or whatever?"

"Yeah. Girls always like it when I'm straight up with them. *You*, I'm not sure about."

Christopher stifled his laugh. "Oh, I see. You're doing, like, a thing."

"Yeah, I'm doing a thing."

"Yeah."

"But seriously: Do not text her for a while," he cautioned. "Women don't like to be ignored, but somehow worse is when you try to play games. Just leave it be. If you start something, even if she responds very nicely, it'll either peter out because you don't actually have anything you want to talk to her about, and then you'll be hellishly depressed all week, or it'll be a nice conversation that leads you into a position where you feel compelled to ask her out even though you haven't done enough to prepare for that yet."

"Ugh. Yes, I suppose you're right."

"Good," he said. "Now, because we both know that you're going to end up texting her anyway, let's go over what you might say."

"Hahaha," Christopher burst out. "Yes. Good."

"Yes. So, what might you say?"

"Well, I thought I'd start with, 'Hi, how'd it go on Friday?'"

"Alright." *What does that even mean? Do more.*

"And then she'd say something like, 'It was fun! How was the rest of barhopping?'"

"Okay." *Can't assume that, but okay.*

"And then...I don't know what to say," Christopher said.

"Right."

"What should I say?"

"Hmm. How about, 'It was fun, we moved from Lucky's to wherever – name the places – talk about something funny or noteworthy that happened, 'We missed you out there,'" he said.

"Hmm. That's pretty good."

"Well, it's alright."

"Why would you suggest it if you don't like it?" Christopher asked.

"Well, I don't think you should text her at all."

"Yes, I *know* that, fool. But I'm either going to be unhappy that I texted her or unhappy that I didn't, and I'd rather regret doing something than regret being a coward."

"It's not cowardly to neglect forcing conversation with someone with whom you have nothing to discuss," he said.

"Heh. Yeah. But, I mean, I have nothing else to care about right now."

"Enjoy yourself for that, then," he said, envious even for the prospect of peace.

"I can't."

"Yes, I know, *dog*."

"So, what's a better thing to say?" Christopher demanded.

"Well, I wasn't dissatisfied with my suggestion because there's a better one out there. I think some variation of that is your best bet. But I think a truly great bet would be waiting a few days to text or call her at all."

"But I don't *want* to wait," *Swingers* dialogue hanging close to Christopher's lips.

"Nevertheless," he answered, "You'd do well to trust Lords Favreau and Vaughn and *wait* – that is, if you prefer to ever hear some amorous or intriguing reply from this girl."

"Perhaps you're right."

"Oh, I'm right."

"However…" Christopher mumbled.

They were silent for a while, and he laughed under his breath. "Yes. So, anyway – what are you texting her?"

"Haha…I see." Nothing surprised Christopher, but he liked to let people believe it had.

"Yes, I may be reeling, but my powers are not wholly diminished. There was no way you weren't texting her. Did you say what I said you should say?"

"Something like it."

"Very good," he said. He still laid in bed, head rested on an extra pillow, neck contorted uncomfortably enough to keep him awake.

"Thank you."

"Don't mention it. We'll add it to your tab."

"Well, I'll let you know what she says, if anything," Christopher said, sympathy hunting.

"I'm sure it'll be fine. Just don't force anything and don't get upset if it doesn't immediately become some spellbinding conversation."

"No promises."

"I know." He laughed with the little breath allowed in his folded position.

Christopher maneuvered away from his own problems. "So, would you like to discuss—"

"No, no I wouldn't."

"So, you're just going to keep waiting?"

"Yes, it's all I have the strength to do," he said.

"Well, I think it's valiant and honorable, and I hope one day she sees that."

"That's kind of you. I don't know what she's thinking about, but she's smarter than me. I'm just not what she needs right now, I guess. And, obviously, I've had to consider that she's not exercising the same restraint."

"What would you do if you found that out for sure?" Christopher said.

"I don't know."

"Would you ask out that girl from the coffee shop?"

"Heh. You jest, but being honest, I don't think I could ever ask anyone else out."

"You say that, but—"

"I just don't yearn that way anymore," a silly theater filled his deepened voice.

Christopher laughed for the exercise and pressed him, "So, you're not whipped, you're just a knight of the Frowntable?"

"How *dare* you, impudent knave!"

"Haha!"

"But, yes, that's me. I don't know what the right thing to do is, so I guess I'll just keep myself ashamed and do nothing. Whatever she's up to isn't my business until she chooses to make it so." *I do believe that, I do.*

"Do you actually believe that?"

"I'm just trying to breathe," he said.

"I know, and I'm sorry, old boy."

"Me too."

A more earnest laugh followed from Christopher. "So, you did want to discuss it."

"You...*you!*"

"Ha! And, on that note, I must be going."

"Oh? Where must you to be going?" he asked.

"I've been invited to play trivia, and I don't feel like wallowing anymore, myself."

"Ah, very good. Yes, go forth and wallow no more."

"I shall try," Christopher said defiantly.

"Mmm."

"And you?"

"Well, I haven't gotten much done today. I'll probably try to put a few pages together." He wiggled under his blanket and decided in advance not to pull it away but to stay warm and unoccupied beneath.

"Very good."

"Yes."

"Try to hang in there," Christopher always said.

"No promises."

"Indeed. Speak to you later."

He hung up and found his notebook across the bed, opened it, and scanned the pages of musical metaphor he'd buried some ruminations on autumn in hours before. He was proud of the feeling and the rhythm of it but began to think it was too dramatic. After a few minutes he raised his pen to the page and thrust two angry slashes across the pages in an "X." He wrote across it in huge letters, *Junk*. He threw the notebook back over the bed. It landed on the edge before slowly sliding and falling to the ground. Half asleep, he wandered waking dreams most of the night. In one he was a Trojan soldier, defending the right of his prince to love Helen – because she loved him back. In another he was Lancelot, risking life and limb and taking on exile just to love Guinevere, whether they were together or not. He had long since written as much about that as he'd hoped to. Years before, he'd have shot up to add those dreams to a cleaner notebook. But in his dreams he remained, sharpening his heart more finely than the sword. That much could not be lost to him: he had loved ferociously.

"Hi there," he said.

"Funny seeing you here," she grinned.

"It is."

"How are you feeling?"

They walked down the hallway of his old apartment and stood in the doorway of the bedroom with half a dozen uncertain feet between them. "Not bad. And you?"

"Better now." She grinned wider and approached him slowly.

Without warning he took Sara by the small of her back and pulled her into his arms and they kissed. It went on for a while. Should it be any different when you've waited months to see someone?

"Wow."

"Wow…" she agreed.

"It feels so good to be with you," he tumbled, catching his breath.

"How do you like it around here?"

"I like it a lot," he said.

"Think you'll choose it?"

"I don't know. It's an expensive neighborhood, but it is beautiful."

"It's worth it. It'll be worth it to be near you," she said.

"I know. I hope I can. The rep said I could look around a bit and just left," he laughed.

"How long do you think we have?"

"A few hours. I'll have to be on a train home by five or so to be back before dark."

"'A few hours' is great. Want to get lunch?"

"Can we skip lunch?" she asked.

"Of course we can."

They wrapped up one another and settled on the empty carpeted floor. It was a scene they'd replayed for dozens of reunions, now replayed in his notebooks once a week or so.

154

Twenty

He emerged from the steam of the shower, dried, and performed a series of obsessive-compulsive hygienic rituals, opened every window in the apartment, and lit candles. He found a fresh black t-shirt in his drawer, underwear and socks, dark wash jeans, a powder blue shirt – *no, a black one; no, the blue one*. He rolled the sleeves up, slipped his sneakers on, and began to rearrange and organize the piles of DVDs and books all over the living room onto shelves. He left the stack of notebooks as they were, an effort to indicate that he was, in fact, very busy and always working.

There was a knock on the door.

The heightened anxiety he had predicted for the moment did not appear. Very matter-of-factly, he glided to the door, looked through the peep hole, confirmed that it was Lily, turned the knob, and swung it open.

"Hi there."

"Hi," she said. Her hair was held back in a loose ponytail, bangs dangling over her ears. She wore a baggy, plaid sweater over a white t-shirt, loose jeans, and old, grey running sneakers.

"Glad to see you again," he said.

"You too."

She paced slowly into the living room and looked around. "I guess I shouldn't be surprised by the books."

"You can be. I still am."

"It's all very *you*." She kept studying.

"Thank you, I hope."

"I guess it's not a bad thing," she teased, grinning. "What're we watching?"

"A few good options."

"Like what?"

"Let's see here…" He walked to the shelf of DVDs and searched for something sophisticated and challenging. '"Thirteen Seconds?'"

"Boring."

"Hmm… 'Green Ritual?'"

"*So* boring."

"Uh, 'Depresso?'"

"Overplayed."

"Sorry," he sighed and laughed.

"Why all the serious mind-benders?"

"I just figured, we've had interesting conversations, I didn't want to suggest something stupid."

"I think I prefer stupid things," she said.

"Stupid things like 'Hot Fuzz?'" His fingers glided to the end of the top row and pulled the case out halfway.

"If by 'stupid,' you mean the most genius film of the twenty-first century thus far."

"As a matter of fact, that's exactly what I mean," he smiled.

"Good, perfect."

He slid the DVD into the player and waited for the menu to appear. "Please, make yourself at home. Can I offer you a drink? Tea, coffee?"

"Do you have any dark liquor?"

"You must have read my dust jacket," he said with a smirk.

"Heh. Maybe I did."

"Scotch okay?" He held up a bottle from the kitchen counter.

Without looking back, she said, "Whatever," she smiled sheepishly because 'whatever' was very important.

He brought two rocks glasses from the cabinet above the fridge, filled them each with lots of ice, and poured dishonestly modest portions. He had had two before his shower.

"Thank you."

"Of course." He hit PLAY on the remote, took a swig from his glass, and sat on the couch opposite her.

Simon Pegg, adorned in heavily armored London Police regalia, marched toward the camera's fourth wall through a long hallway and then stopped to announce his opening monologue.

"He's just perfect in the exaggerated seriousness," she said.

"That's why I love this so much. It's a great premise, but it also lends itself to his development right out of the gate."

Her brow furrowed. "It's not even about the parody. It's just implicitly funny."

Definitely. "I love the series of amazing things he's good at, next," he said, Police Constable Nicholas Angel listing his accolades and heroics on screen.

"It breaks the fourth wall right away, not just with him looking into the camera, but him giving us direct exposition that's absurdly on-the-nose for its usefulness," she matched his speed.

Half an hour into the film Lily turned to him, an arm rested over the back of the couch, and interrupted, "Can we just talk instead?" She gulped the last of her glass.

"I'd prefer that," he said, unsure if he really would.

"Can I have another?"

"Nice work on that, Ernest." He reached to the coffee table and refilled her glass.

"And you are who, exactly, Mother Theresa?" She accepted her glass, then extended it back and shook it at him. "A little more, please…"

He laughed along. *Well, so long as she's testing what's appropriate…* "No, I don't know anything about missionaries."

"Woah, woah…"

He went red – though that, too, may have been the scotch. "Sorry, didn't mean to—"

"I'm kidding," and she cackled.

"Jeez…Okay, more for me, too." He poured.

"So, you don't believe in God, I presume?"

He laughed. "Where'd that come from?"

"Just being direct – no tip-toeing."

"Hmm. Well, only when it's not a pejorative," he said.

"You don't seem to mind being a lot more of a cliché than you want to be. Isn't it either always or never a pejorative?"

His relent came with a magnanimous smile. "Ouch. Give me a moment to let that sting fade. You don't seem so absolute about anything to me."

"I'm not, but you are," she grinned.

"You know, I was just thinking how I've seldom known quicker whips," he said.

Her grin widened. "Know a lot about whip craft, do you?"

If he could have reddened more, he would have. "You're deflecting."

"You already were."

"From all his thinking on the subjects of gods and faith he gathered," I only live by the knowledge I really have."

She thought of his answer carefully, then countered, "Well, I believe because it doesn't feel as if I need evidence to."

"You don't. Just depends on what either one does for you."

"So, what *do* you believe?" she pressed, leaning further across the couch.

"There's energy, there's spirituality, there's lots of things we don't understand. I don't get bothered by the things I don't understand. Maybe that's just because there aren't many of them—"

159

"Ha! I believe in those, too. But it is comforting and directing to have a sense of implicit meaning that I share with other people. It makes sense to me." She sipped her second.

"Whatever works."

"Then as long as we're on the unmentionables…Politics. Go," she led.

"Well, obviously, the whole American government has to be torn down."

She had been holding her breath and exhaled hard. "Whew…That's a relief." They both laughed. "It's all gotta go. There's no real freedom. There's clearly some kind of conspiracy in charge of everything."

He brightened and sat up. "Well, I don't know if I'd give them so much credit as a conspiracy, but clearly, the ones in charge of the government keep sabotaging the parts that distinguish it from autocratic and theocratic dictatorships." He grasped his glass firmly, forgetting about his sipping regiment, and folded his legs underneath him, turning completely towards her.

"The whole thing. Torn down."

"Shattered."

"Dug up and thrown away," she said.

"Burnt to ash and scattered to the breeze," he said, louder.

"How do we do it?"

"Carefully, one subtle movement at a time."

She put her grin back on. "A few laws changed here, a few protests there."

"Inching towards flames."

"Carving out the foundation for something new."

They had been inching closer across the couch with each line, sipping in turns as the other spoke. Suddenly they were quiet – they had gotten too close, smiles and postures looking very stupid and breaths getting hot.

Lily leaned back and straightened up. "You know, I...don't want to sleep with you."

He hadn't realized how red he'd gotten. He took another deep breath through his lower teeth, then exhaled loudly and spoke, "Phew," moving the back of his hand across his forehead.

Laughing, she doubled down, "I'm being serious. This is great, I'm just not looking—"

"Neither am I," he interrupted. "Without knowing how this would go, 'my place at 7 on a Sunday' would have kind of been a terrible plan if I meant this to be a date."

"I didn't think you were shallow or anything, I just thought, hey, all guys..."

"I know, I get it, but seriously, I wasn't thinking that way at all."

She kicked her sneakers off and brought her legs under her torso. "Why can't people just...?"

"Like you said, I'm not interested in being a total cliché anyway," he said proudly.

"Heh. Neither am I."

"It's just nice to be the same."

"The same is great," she said.

He looked deep and long into her eyes and through impressive drunkenness that she reflected, managed to describe to himself, *wow: this evening has been one of the best in so long – just talking, and talking about everything. And she is beautiful. But, for a hundred reasons, I don't want her. If we could just keep talking without any other expectations, that would be tremendous.*

And he got his wish. They kept talking, pouring, laughing, and doubling down on everything that was happening around them. Notions of intimacy or romance could not penetrate the shield wall of this titanic diplomacy.

"Okay, twenty questions," she challenged.

"Okay. Have you got one already?"

"No, no – not normal Twenty Questions. We just ask twenty questions," she corrected, and slunk down to the floor beside the coffee table, cross-legged as a wave of semi-serious focus washed over her expression.

"Ah, okay. I reserve the right to answer in half-truths and wishful fictions," he followed to the floor, sitting opposite her.

"That's no fun."

"Fine. I suppose I'm drunk enough to suspend my belief in myself."

"Ha! First question: When did you decide you were a writer?"

"Seriously? Free reign to embarrass and dig into me with a scalpel, and you go for the late-night television softball?"

"You're not answering."

He exhaled and breathed in through clenched lower teeth. "When I was five."

"Five?"

"Five. My turn—"

She barked, "No, no, no. That's not a full answer."

162

"Fine. My folks are writers. We wrote short stories together from the time I was five, so I never really decided I was a writer. I just...always have been." A flare of drunken heat flashed through him.

"That's too cool."

"Well, it's enough for my turn," his eyes moved away from her and to the fridge beyond as he thought. "What is your favorite country you've traveled to and why?"

"The 'and why' is another question," she said.

"No, it's not, come on."

"It is – and I'm going to have to charge you for two questions. A shame, really, 'cause I probably would have naturally answered the 'why' without you saying anything."

"Jesus."

"Didn't you say you were competitive?" She raised her fists and turned her torso to a fighting stance, her legs still crossed. "We're not going to be able to remain friends if you're not competitive."

"No, I'm very competitive – that's why I'm pissed right now."

"Let your guard down, huh? Or didn't think you had much competition here?"

"The former," he teased with his eyebrows.

"We can chalk it up to the scotch if it makes you feel better."

"Relax, will ya? You win this round, count it for two questions."

"I know; and we will. My favorite country I've visited is Greece."

"*That's* too cool," he mimicked.

"The sun, the water, the feeling of isolation even in a crowd. It's very special."

"For two questions you've got to give me a little more than that."

"Did I say I was done yet?" An almost believable front of anger barely made it past her drunk swooning.

"Woah..." he mocked with a fearful tremble.

She chuckled. "Now *you* relax. Some people don't like Mediterranean, but I do, so the food's not a problem. Some people don't like not being able to communicate easily, but I like having a challenge and learning some of the language, so that's not a problem. And some people think that seeing famous tourist attractions somehow cheapens vacations – they just want to see the secret, local holes-in-the-walls. But I wanted to see the Parthenon and Delphi and Santorini, so I did, and they were great."

"That's what I'd see there. Attractions are attractive f."

"Your turn. Hmm. What's your favorite movie?"

"You've got to narrow that down a bit," sipping slower than usual, he considered getting water for the two of them, then forgot about it.

"Nope, you have to choose."

"Well, the criteria are different for comedies and dramas—"

She interjected, "I know, that's why I'm making you choose."

"You know, this level of competition isn't actually healthy," he quipped, then poured a shot's worth of iced scotch down his gullet in one go and exhaling.

"Your face doesn't flinch when you gulp this stuff real hard." Looking to the floor, she was almost sullen. "How much of it do you drink?"

He smiled. "Enough not to flinch – and enough not to be distracted by your question."

"Competition makes the world go 'round."

"'Superbad.'"

"Ha!" she burst into laughter. He smiled meekly in response. "You're being serious?"

"Actually, I wasn't – but as I think about it, maybe I am. Of course, it's incredibly funny, but I also think it's very smart, has fun layers, is very self-aware, and it's even heartwarming at the end. But not cheaply like rom-coms and dramas are."

"I was so sure you'd hit me with some 90s cult drama I've never heard of," she said.

"Well, I also had 'Rodger Dodger' on the docket—"

"Heard of it."

"Seen it?" he challenged.

She blushed. *No, that's just the liquor.* "That wasn't the criterion." Sipping, she finally showed a sign of slowing – a brief, almost imperceptible twitch in her glass hand.

"Fine," he pouted, then produced a devilish smirk. "I also thought of the Disney 'Robin Hood.'"

"Stop. The animated one? With animals?"

Perfect. "Yes, the greatest film ever made, un-ironically."

"It actually is," she agreed.

Now they were both wobbly and laughing silly at anything, he noticed. "We'll have to have a whole other conversation about that."

"We will."

"Your turn—"

"Nope." Giggling at something she kept to herself, she planted the glass on the table, turned perpendicular to him, and stretched her legs out.

"You didn't say my two questions counted at the same time," he sloshed, resting his head on the seat of the couch behind him. The room spun when he closed his eyes for an extra moment.

"I think that was implied," she said. What, did you think you were going to save the second one for later and I'd forget about it?"

"I had hoped that might happen, yeah."

"'Nice try'…is what I'd say if that had been clever," she said, laughing to herself again as she reached the tips of her fingers to her toes.

"Ouch." He laughed along, considering why after a couple of hours in his living room, Lily was more comfortable in it than he was.

Okay, we've sized one another up. She's still trying to outwit me, and do it stylishly, and I've given up on that and am letting her play the game to an audience. That should leave me half a step ahead and—

"Third question. Can I read something you've written?"

Ah, shit. "I'd really rather you didn't."

"Why?"

He ruffled his chin and wrapped his thumb and forefinger around it. "Well, I don't want you to call the authorities and tell them there's an insane person at 494 Pico Ave, Apartment 5B, who's plotting to overthrow the government and install a social committee that makes political decisions by objectifying the wits and attractiveness of the voters."

"Haha! Seriously, I want to read something. What are you working on that's new?"

"I really don't have much to read," he said, cheekily eyeing the pile of scrap ideas next to them on the coffee table. He couldn't tell if he wanted her to read something out of pride or if he wanted her nowhere near that stuff out of shame.

"Very funny." She followed his eyes and reached for the stack. "I'm just going to take the first thing I see then."

"Wait, no, don't!" he said, laughing along with his semi-serious warning, he was drunk enough to crawl the three feet between them across the floor, feigning to stop her.

"This looks interesting…" she snickered at him, holding him back with a hand on his chest; folding back a top page of scribbles and crossed-out nonsense. She bowed over the table and read aloud while he listened.

> You don't have to age too much for wonderful things to stop being exciting. Give the time a little more juice and even toiled, earned things seem to stop being rewarding. I have to imagine, at this rate, that by thirty, even patiently suffered things will stop being relieving. I can't guess what there will be left to feel after that.

She skipped a few pieces and started again at random, still holding his chest back while he flailed his arms in a make-believe effort to stop her.

> *Is nobody bothered by how cheapening and ungallant the phrases "a really good fuck" and "a really bad fuck" are? I know I'm old-fashioned, but is there much hope of feeling some romantic or lasting connection to an experience by referring to it that way? Is the timely cost of a few more syllables really too high to say, instead, "an intimate reveal better forgotten," or "a carnal exchange that was over entirely too soon?" Is fucking really the part of language we want to make terse and unimaginative or to outsource to the basest sentiments we have? Isn't style important to anyone?*

He could tell that she could tell he wanted her to read it and either attack him or comfort him, and he could tell she liked that. She flipped a page, found more scribbles, and flipped another.

> *I do not believe anything could be more important than my bookshelves. My grandmother was a schoolteacher, and she once gave to me a very old, very sturdy pine bookshelf that her classroom was getting rid of. I stripped it of dozens of layers of latex paint, each representing years of first and second graders learning to read. It is so strong, the pine uncovered at the bottom so smooth and plain*

that I keep all my favorite books on it. But the shelf matters more than the books on it. Not because I re-made the shelf and didn't make the books — though that ownership distinction is an interesting thought — but because I like the shelf. The shelf is absent content, despite being full of it, and I cannot accuse it of anything. I feel equally empathetic about old fans that are left on, overheating, for hours, or an old mattress that's gone saggy in the middle. Inanimate things that have no sensation or opinion...they are always honest and deserve better than they get.

"Sheesh," she finally said after a quiet while.

"What?" He was less nervous than he'd usually be upon review, thanks to the liquor.

"Well, I think you could use some work refining this third one," she said coyly. "You're doing too many things and don't get deep enough."

Great care was taken to ignore the Freud in her review. "You're right. I hadn't worked on it because I was going to scrap it."

"You scrap too many things instead of working through them," she said, pointing at the basket of crumpled legal papers across the room.

"I promise I don't — they're irredeemably bad."

She rolled her eyes and carefully placed his pages back on the table. "Well, these other two...they're definitely very good."

"Really?"

"Yes, incredible, actually." There was a breathy resignation in her voice that seemed to mean she was telling the truth. "This one about things you can't feel with more age: it's perfectly sad but without giving up. I think too many people write about wanting to give up. I like this because you're just saying something's bad without being suicidal over it or something."

"Okay." He focused his eyes at an angle that requisitioned more praise.

"And this second one, about the phrase 'a good fuck...' It's very funny, but I have to admit I can't be as angry about it as you."

"Why, do you use the phrase?" he asked.

"No, I just wouldn't hang out with anyone that did, so I don't have anyone to direct my anger towards."

"Haha, that's very preppy and critical of you. I like it."

"Thanks – I'm definitely known for being very preppy and critical," she said.

They laughed, poured another round, asked more questions, and, at around 2 AM, fell asleep, her curled up across the couch, him leaning his neck against the edge of it.

Morning

"Hey."

He groggily looked up to see Lily, tying her hair up, buttoning her shirt.

"Good morning," he mumbled. He looked again at her semi-buttoned blouse, then at his messy overshirt. "We didn't...?" he pretended.

"No," she said, giggling. "We decidedly did not."

"Good," he said, letting out a sigh and a chuckle.

"I'm a bit disappointed you don't remember the evening."

"Miss Preppy and Critical likes 'Hot Fuzz.' I'm not so far gone yet."

"Haha, fair enough," she said, struggling with her next button.

"Where are you rushing off to?"

"Well, I have my class this morning."

"Oh, of course, I'm sorry I forgot that."

171

"So, I will see you another time?" It was rhetorical but she wasn't laughing yet.

"Obviously – but wait a moment. Can you give me five minutes?"

"Why?"

"Well, I thought we could get coffee," he said.

"Oh, heh. Sure. But I have to be efficient if that's okay. We tend to talk for two hours without noticing it."

"For that short?"

"Yeah."

"Okay, heh. I'll be quick. One second." He rushed into the bathroom and tore his clothes off. He brushed his teeth and his hair in record time, then replaced his black t-shirt and the rest, chose new jeans and a new overshirt, and fetched a notepad, pen, his wallet, and phone from various places.

She tapped her watchless wrist. "That was nearly six minutes – I was about to leave."

"Sorry."

"I'm kidding."

"I know – I meant sorry you didn't just leave," he bobbed his head side to side as he teased.

She punched his arm and started for the door. "Asshole."

"Coffee."

"Yep."

Out his door, down the steps, across the street and into the Coffee Bean, they marched. In the line, they exchanged criticisms of the overcomplicated orders that preceded them, in hushed voices. They ordered their coffee and tea.

"You groan," she said, sipping on the lid of her hot mocha, never looking at him.

"Huh?"

"In your sleep. You groan every little while."

"You snore."

"Fuck off." She sipped again while he laughed with himself.

"When's your class?" he pointed to the clock above the barista station.

"Oh, shit. Yeah, I'm gonna be late."

"Go on, get outta here."

"Let's hang out again," she said, this time almost a question.

"Obviously."

"Alright, I'll call you."

He laughed. "Yeah, you call this time; or else it'll start getting weird."

"Wouldn't want that," she answered with another of her eye rolls, but she lingered.

"You going or what?"

"See ya." She reached her arms around him and hugged him. It was half uncomplicated kindness and half pity for a sad, dying creature. He turned to find a table and she left.

He sat down at a corner table and landed his notepad on it. Flipping to a new page, he sipped on his tea. For once, recently, his problem wasn't an absence of ideas but an abundance of them through which he could not sift.

Sometimes, simple kindness can breathe life
into dying flesh, with no wantonness or hidden

ambition. Sometimes, you can be wrong about absolutely everything, no matter how hard you argue or how badly you want something else. And in realizing these changes, you can change yourself.

Damn, he thought – *total bullshit again*.

In his pocket, his phone vibrated. *Here comes Christopher – naturally*. He pulled the ringing from within and in a single motion tapped "Accept," only noticing the name on the screen in his periphery as the speaker reached his mouth and he said, "Hello?"

"Hey," Sara said.

"H-hi."

"I'm sure you weren't expecting to hear from me."

"Well," he stuttered, "I always like to hear from you."

"I think we should talk," she said quickly.

"Okay, what's new—"

"Not now," she interrupted. "I have work. Sometime this week?"

"Uh, yes, of course, just let me know."

"Okay."

"Great," he said, calm as he could.

After a silence she answered, in a higher pitch, "You sound good."

"You too."

"Thanks."

"Hmm." There was plenty more he'd have wanted to say, if only he'd thought of it.

"Well, I'll speak to you soon."

174

"Yeah, sounds good."

"Bye."

"Bye."

***

"If it weren't you, I'd be sure this was made up," Christopher said.

He paced the primal space between the coffee table and the kitchen counter. "I still feel as if it's made up."

"I know."

"It sounds like something you'd sardonically wish upon me as punishment for not being as much of a sleaze as you find entertaining," he said.

"Ha. Actually, yeah, it does. In fact, it pretty much is what I said would happen."

"What?"

"I told you; you'd end up having to make a choice," a delighted Christopher explained.

"There is no choice. Sara called. She wants to talk. We're not currently together, so that means she wants to get back together."

"Maybe. Or maybe she just wants to be nice and see how you're doing, then reinforce that she doesn't want to be together now," Christopher said.

"Maybe."

"And then keep delaying it."

"Okay, point taken," he said, pacing faster. "But more likely, she's calling for a real reason. Like she wants to get back together."

"I suppose. But is that what you'll choose?"

"There is no choice. Seriously. I'm not interested in Lily. We had a blast – I think we'll be great friends," he waited for an interruption that didn't come. "I don't know why you can't understand this."

"I don't know how many times I can use the phrase, 'let me get this straight' with the same person in one month – you must be going for the record," Christopher attacked. "But, let me get this straight: you met a woman with whom you have a great connection, love her company, she goes out of her way to give you her phone number, you invite her over to watch a movie and talk as friends, you end up drinking and talking about your personal lives, you fall asleep across from each other in front of the TV, and you make plans to see each other again...And you're telling me you have no feelings beyond friendship?"

"That's what I'm telling you."

"Then why are you bringing this up?"

Knowing it was a purely performative measure, he scoffed. "I told you the two things that happened. I thought they were ironic, and I figured you'd react like this and it's funny."

"No."

"No?"

"You would have told me, perhaps, but you wouldn't be so frantic about it," Christopher said. "You weren't expecting the call from Sara, so you were going to call me and tell me what happened last night and this morning anyway. But now, you're calling and presenting the two events to me as an entertaining query."

"It's not a query. It's just the two things that just happened in sequence."

"I don't think so."

"You're insane."

"*You're* insane," Christopher almost yelled.

"God dammit. You're creating this problem in my brain, so I think about it and get confused."

"If it works, you were already confused."

"I'm not confused, he said."

"I think you are."

"I'm not. I've waited a long time."

"Okay." Rarely did Christopher believe the things he said, even on good days.

"What should I say to her?" he asked.

"Suddenly you're the one unable to speak to women."

"Yes, I am. This is serious."

"Just wait to see what she says. You always tell me not to overreact and get paranoid." It was Christopher's impression of him. "Just see what she wants to say whenever you talk to her."

"Remind me to get you a guest spot on 'Dr. Phil.'"

"That would be great actually, thank you."

"Christ. I'll talk to you later." He hung up.

> It's sobering to have everything you're
> thinking about unravel or emerge at once as
> they tend to do. It's sobering because it's
> overwhelming and focusing, yes, but also
> because having so many concerns at once can

bring you to the point of drinking so much that the slightest shock renders you sober.

It can also help you reflect on your ambitions for sobriety if you have them, or permanent drunkenness if you have them. If the bottleneck has a permanent fixture in your palm, and you're concerned about, well, death – or, at the very least, the absence of life – it cannot be recommended more strongly that you feel the brunt of three or four life-altering trials all at once. If cutting yourself while nursing another wound can release endorphins that relieve some of the pain, it's a bit like that. When you cut, you're risking your safety. When you face emotionally obfuscating reconstructions of your feelings, it becomes harder to notice the bottle – at the risk of neglecting whether you drink more. Okay, look, it's not recommended for everybody.

Sometimes, you can start to realize that you have a problem slowly. Even if stopping cold turkey is in the cards, realizing that you need to is another matter. You become accustomed to greater and greater degrees of effect, longer and longer times affected, and less and less of the view through the window of your former self, functional, excitable, driven. You can become consumed without realizing you've done more than dip a toe in the water, and pretty easily.

Sometimes, you can become aware of this more quickly, like when the other members of a wedding party begin to refer to you as the "world's foremost expert on paint thinners."

The Boxer or the Bag

"Well, that does it, then," he said, squeezing her hands between his a little tighter.

"Does what?" Sara said.

"I'm definitely, completely in love with you."

She politely chuckled. "I really like you, a lot...But I think...Let's slow down a little bit."

"Of course."

"Like, I've loved this conversation just as much as you have."

"Mmm..." he could hardly focus.

"But we met two hours ago."

"Yeah, I'm sorry. I don't mean to be fast. I'm just certain."

She giggled again. "I can tell, and it's sweet."

Their eyes hadn't unlocked the whole night. It was a sensation he was totally unfamiliar with. He was utterly sober but with no control over his mind or body. He kept replaying the previous hour – particularly when he reached for her hand and led her to the front of the stage, to slow-dance to the awful rendition of a Counting Crows song offered by a very dramatic cover band. He hadn't given a thought of hesitation to embarrassing himself in front of hundreds of people for making such a dramatic moment the scene of such a dramatic realization; or, worse, embarrassing himself in front of her as he fumbled around, unsure how to dance. And then she'd held him during all his favorite parts of the song as if they'd already lived a few lifetimes together, and she knew the ways he wanted to live and die better than he.

Or before that, when he'd failed to keep her out of his periphery for his whole set – she'd moved closer and closer to the stage until she was right in front of him. By his third song he'd begun staring back at her exclusively, probably to the dismay of the rest of the crowd. He hadn't missed a note of singing or playing. He had felt a new sort of tingling through his hands the whole time.

And now they stood back on the patio, the thick breath of summer exhausting into a deep cold in his chest – there must be some spell he could put over her so that she'd never leave.

"Well, I sense this soiree is filing out," he said, their hands still folded together as they sized up one another's bodies and faces without apology.

"A shame," she teased.

"I'd really like to see you again soon."

"I'd like that," she said with her eyes answering a call from her side. "My friend is telling me it's time to go, and she's my ride. Do you have my number?"

He wondered how he could possibly have her number. He was thrilled she was still nervously playing the game, too.

"No, sadly."

"Well, we should remedy that – can I see your phone?"

"Sure—"

No sooner had he agreed than she'd added her number to it.

"Thank you."

"So, you know, call me, or something."

"Heh…I definitely will."

"Okay. Great to finally meet you. See ya 'round…"

"Yeah, likewise. Goodbye for now." She finally let go of his hands and turned to leave the club. Before she could take a second step away, he reached for her nearest hand to stop her.

"Wait."

She turned back to him. "Yes?" Those eyes were sadists. Unyielding killers.

"I j-just…wanted to ask you," he stuttered – again unlike him – and lowered his head to kiss her hand. "And sorry, I'm a bit old-fashioned." He looked up to her eyes again. "Would you mind if I wrote you something?"

"What?"

"Would you mind if I wrote something for you or to you?"

"I mean…I can't stop you," she smiled.

"Okay."

"I've got to go!"

"Of course, I'm sorry." He let go, and she disappeared through the crowd that streamed through the front doors.

Suddenly a thin, excited figure appeared beside him, smirking. "Hey, who was that?"

"Oh, hey, Dave. Just a girl."

"I bet. Hmm. Ready to head out?"

"Sure," he laughed back. Got to load out?"

"Yeah, waiting on your amps."

"Ah, yes, apologies."

Before he'd plopped down in the passenger seat of Dave's silver van, their gear weighing it down to the asphalt, the urge to call her overtook him.

It was inexcusable. He couldn't possibly do this. He had to resist a while at least. How desperate and stupid would that look?

No, he thought: This is it. This is all that matters. For the hundredth time tonight, I don't give a shit what I look like. I have to keep talking to her. Maybe, she'll like it. He searched his contacts and started typing when he found her.

"Hi there."

"Hi. Who is this?"

"Oh, I'm sorry – I guess I shouldn't have expected to be the only guy who fell in love with you tonight."

On Getting Off

"You're crazy, you know that."

"Crazy about," he glanced at the black-and-white essay printed on the tiny desk in front of him, "'Sartre, Nietzsche, and the New Nothing.'"

Lily sneered through a fast series of blinks before returning her attention to the front of the hall.

"You know, you should be flattered. I swore off this shit at least two lifetimes ago," he muttered. They'd sat in the row second from the back, a few seats in. Neither of them remembered why he was attending her Thursday afternoon 'Philosophy 238: Contemporary Vs. Modern' lecture, but that curiosity had quickly been reduced to a secondary effort, behind preserving his anonymity. Dr. Rosen, a tall and gangly man in his fifties, with a round, pleasant smile but narrow, stern eyes, had enforced most of his daily regiment seriously. Inviting an unenrolled trespasser wouldn't do Lily's grade point average any good. Maybe that was half his motivation.

"I'm feeling all sorts of un-flattered right now," she hissed.

He noticed her shrivel and slump further into her desk and he chortled silently. "There are, what, a hundred or so kids in here? Even if he remembers you all, he won't even *detect* me."

She glared peripherally without moving her head. "He will if you don't shut the fuck up."

He smirked and tilted his head down to the hand-out.

"Good afternoon, everyone," Rosen piped up from his seat in the distance. He hadn't looked up from the planner, calendar, and other notes scattered on his desk.

A chorus of "good afternoon" lazily responded, mostly from the seats nearest him.

"Well, don't everyone erupt in excitement at once," he joked back, lame. A rumbling of polite laughs warmed the room. "Alright then, heh. Let's get right into it today." He stood abruptly from the desk and raised his head, leaning into the attention he'd suddenly commanded from the whole of the hall. "And, Mr. Jorgen," he eyed a kid in the front row who looked nineteen or twenty with a kind, if assertive, cynicism, "if you're planning on replying with quotations and context clues like we're in second-period junior high, by all means, do – but give everyone else a turn."

Young Mr. Jorgen went red but nodded as he laughed along with a few classmates. *Fuck. Son-of-a-bitch actually knows them.*

"So," Rosen continued, "What can we say connects Sartre and Nietzsche, to start? Miss Parkins," he pointed and walked with shy purpose towards a girl in the second row, "Go ahead, please."

She'd read. "What I enjoyed most about Sartre is that he insists there isn't some sort of pre-set, fabricated experience – or, core, was it? – in human life. Not so much 'nurture before nature,' so to speak. But that our priorities and interpretations of experience are unique to us –"

"Yes," Rosen cut her off as politely as he could. "He rejects the idea that the human 'essence,' if you will, is prescribed. Interesting phrasing. And what about this view do you feel is shared by Nietzsche? Remember, Nietzsche believed in a clear effort towards the individual but also referred to the common man as the 'rabble,' rather than promoting that individualism towards him."

"Well," Miss Parkins sounded proud of staving off impatience while being interrupted, "His version of the 'individual' rejects pre-determined, self-defining concepts like the soul."

"Very interesting connection, Miss Parkins. Would anyone like to add to that, or challenge it?"

He'd been half listening, sensing a distant value in the discussion but too busy deciding what sort of cheeky note to pass to Lily while she leaned forward, intently listening. He finally settled on, *In the whole big, bad world, I still can't figure how anyone gets off on this…*

Her eyes were already rolling as he passed the folded, torn notebook page under the profile of their desks and into her slowly outstretching hand. They kept rolling while she unfolded the note on her desk, read his comment, and began to add a response.

He scanned the space between them and Rosen, left to right, and felt no suspecting eyes on them. Cupping his chin in one hand, he held out his other below his desk in anticipation.

That's because not everyone enters every social situation fixed only on how they might get off. I wouldn't mind actually hearing this, by the way, her note read.

He tilted his head away from her to feign disappointment, angling his eyes back to search her for anger. She gave a sardonic grin and opened her fist in his direction, waiting for reply.

You probably should *mind having to hear this – but nobody's perfect, so I won't fight with you. I will fight, however, against the idea that any social situation isn't fundamentally, when deconstructed, about getting off. Maybe Nietzsche missed that during his decades in the He-Man-Woman-Haters Club.* He passed it back.

Her answer was quicker. *How do you figure?*

Really? Think it through: Take Dr. Rosen, here. Sweet guy – seems real bright. Probably has a nice family. Why's he teaching here? Presumably to provide the best life he can to them and to himself. Why'd he have the family? Either because he and his partner wanted children or because they had some by accident – either way, someone got off. Mr. Jorgen, down in the front row – why's he so eager to contribute even though everyone can tell he doesn't know what he's talking about? Hoping he'll trip his way into impressing someone, and eventually, he might get off. On and around we go…

Which brings us back to why you're here, she teased, blinking her annoyed face again.

Because the only way I'll ever get off again is if I stop hating myself, and I'm trying to change what my senses are saturated by and get a clearer sense of things.

No need to be so pitifully serious all of a sudden, fella.

It was his turn to roll his eyes as he snatched up the paper, which they'd ceased to bother folding and unfolding with each exchange. *I believe you've invited the same challenge upon yourself, madam. What gets you off about ugly, sexist philosophers and the gradients of selfishness they disguise as insight?* He handed it back, grinning at himself.

No sooner had he set his eyes back to Rosen than he felt a quiet slap against the outside of his hand. Their sheet of paper had run out of space – the darkness of the back of the room had demanded huge, sloppily lined letters – and Lily had started a new one. *Well, I'm not in the game 'cause I think any of them would know best how to use his tongue or forefingers…I needed an elective and didn't want to waste time in something like beekeeping or a business class I'd have hated. Can't blame me for that.*

Suppose I can't. How long is this lecture? Where for lunch?

Done at 2:45. That meant an easy twenty more minutes. It was racing past in their notes. *Hilda's?*

Fine by me. Tea here first, their tea is godawful.

"Excuse me, Miss – up in the back?"

Their eyes froze together in horror and then turned to face Rosen, who peered at them with his body leaning over the front row of seats.

188

She stuttered a moment, but nothing came out right away. "Lily, professor."

"Ah, yes, Lily. Apologies – I haven't learned everyone's names this late in the semester. I try to do my best. In any case, is there something you'd like to share with us? Perhaps about Sartre and existentialism?"

"Um…" she muffled in shame.

"Come to think of it," he paraded his impatience at her, his sweet introductions set off course with the shortest wick, "I don't recognize you, either."

To Lily's dismay, he bowed his head and answered, "Yes, Professor Rosen, my apologies for the disturbance. I realize this is quite unorthodox and inappropriate…"

She looked like she was unsure whether to cry or laugh at his inflated, posh language.

He continued, "I noticed Lily just outside class – we're family friends, you see, and I've been out of the country traveling for several years and only meant to catch up. By the time we'd exchanged phone numbers, you'd begun your lecture and I wished not to rudely interrupt. Sorry, again – I've rather defeated my purpose now." He smiled some very real charm over the abject bullshit.

"Well, now, that is a peculiar situation. Have an interest in modernism, my friend?" Rosen had bought and bitten.

"I do, and I've enjoyed your first hour, albeit unintentionally, very much."

"Well, by all means, keep your seat then," Rosen smiled, both in approval and searching for it. "But, please, the both of you, save your catching up for later."

"Of course, I beg your pardon," he said, sitting back down.

His smirk was as flashy as Lily's grimace. He snatched the scrap of paper from under her fingers as soon as Rosen had turned his back and paced to his desk.

Almost as good getting out of anything as I am getting off with anything.

She huffed, bittered by how readily she resumed. *You're absurd. That could have been horrible. What if I got in trouble?*

I'd never have let you take the blame. What's the big deal? I'm sitting in a room where he's talking, maybe fifty feet from him. If you hadn't made us both laugh by lying about why you're here, nothing would have happened.

I didn't lie – I needed the extra class, and before the last five minutes, I'd thought I'd made a wise decision.

You implied you didn't do it to get off, and therefore, that my theory is incorrect.

Back to this? You're hopeless. Fine. Tell me, how does taking an elective in philosophy mean I just want to get off?

It's this class's fault – I'm being all motivationally analytical! I'll skirt responsibility on this until the end. Well, why are you taking an elective? Because you have a credit requirement, and this course fell into one applicable category or another; you need to take it or one like it to finish your degree, which you need for most careers you'd be interested in; and you need that to be self-sufficient, to have a range of professional and personal boxes checked, including, possibly, having a family. So, yes, eventually, you just wanted to get off.

What if I just want to live in a cottage in the countryside reading for the rest of my life and will be perfectly content not to have children and without getting off for sport?

He grabbed the note back and began to scribble so quickly she may have thought he'd not read it. Before he could finish writing he paused, reread her last entry, and added more.

I won't believe any challenge you give to that, apologies – you're too decisive about what you want for long-term goals to be haphazardly drawn. Oh, you don't want kids? You're free to go off and be a monk, though I can't recommend it as of now. As for sport, haven't you said you're 'generally un-sporty?' Pity.

She'd smirked and bowed to her desk, pen rifling to the scrap, when Rosen called out, "Looks like that's it for today," his first audible words for either of them in some time. The hall emptied in a frenzy. They did their best to get lost in the shuffle to avoid further interrogation.

"You're so O.C.D. it's giving me a run for my own money." Lily parodied his sprinkling of black pepper, napkin folding, and the patterned mixing of his Caesar salad with her bowl of corn chowder, adding improved posture and a downward tilt of the chin, the Victorian charm of which nearly made him throw up.

"Good Christ, I'm nothing like that. I'm gonna be sick."

"I'm very sorry – but also a little thrilled – to be the one to tell you that you're at least twenty percent worse than what I'm depicting."

"Don't be dumb."

"Nothing could ever be as dumb as your little pre-food rituals. Imagine how unsettled you are, but multiply it by, maybe…a billion, to accommodate how much weirder it is to watch *you* do anything."

"Jesus." He smirked, not wholly into the joke, and stabbed at a few lettuce leaves.

"Don't worry. Your secret's safe with me. Especially because I'll never know anyone well enough to feel comfortable admitting that I know you."

"Alright, listen…"

She laughed in anticipation of his fake-serious voice emerging.

"…You're very funny. A very clever girl, and that's just great. I hope you're enjoying yourself. This is all just great."

She laughed between sips of soup, careful never to let her back arch or her elbows touch the table.

"Thank you," he resigned and kept eating.

For a while, he stared out the window of to their small booth at Hilda's. It was the newer sort of diner that serves more than the standard variety, marked by postmodern, industrial décor and lighting that might make those in search of a dingy hangout for cold sandwiches and coffee vaguely unsettled. That was perfect because neither of them wanted to share a fifty-foot radius with that clientele.

He was doing the math again. Here they were, at lunch at an unspectacular, unmemorable diner near her campus. Making rad conversation he could seldom expect from anyone but Christopher. Basking in the comfort of a friendly intimacy that was familiar but still plainly growing, each of them aware of it. While he chewed on another undersized bite, making a mental note to check the distribution of the dressing – which was hellishly uneven – before tossing, next time, he studied her. Her frame suggested diminutive posture, but she always held herself with more force than the brutish people he knew. She was still studying him too - though much less privately.

By what right was he decidedly unattracted to her? He didn't see Sara's reflection in the window where Lily sat. When they spoke, he didn't trace the pair of silver bands on his index and ring fingers between his fingertips, a ritual before he'd let himself speak – at least, not every time. He could hold conversation, not just sprints now but marathons, without interrupting his own thought with a shutter of panic or a stutter of longing. Still, he smiled sadly at Lily as he looked back to acknowledge her, then back out the window. Her allure was academic, her conversation was calculating, and her mannerisms were irksome in their resemblance to his own. These were charms he could appreciate but too easily manage. She was brilliant, but infinitely tamable for one of her own, like himself. Whenever she looked at him, he got the distinct impression that she was similarly unimpressed by his own variation of bizarre.

He chewed at a hangnail on the thumb that rested under his chin.

"You really shouldn't do that, bad for your teeth," she said, falsely shrill.

While he glared at her, she set her spoon down in her soup, brought her hands near her face to examine them, and bit down on the nail of her middle finger. He shifted his glare and nodded back.

"Bad for oral fixation, too," she said between nibbles.

"Why don't we give each other a moment then?"

"What, no 'oral fixation' joke? Your reputation hangs so delicately!" she whisper-yelled.

"I'm all sorts of ridiculous and improper, but I'm not so obvious. Or crass."

"That's your real problem, I think."

"You think I should be crasser?" he asked.

"No, I think you're so caught up trying not to be a cliché that you've gone and plopped yourself knee deep in the worst pits of it I've ever seen."

"Have I?"

"In fact, if you were a little dumber, a little cuter, or a little poorer, I'd find it halfway charming," she teased, looking everywhere else.

His eyebrow shot up to accuse. "That's all it takes for you, huh?"

"Hey."

"Ha. Do you really feel that way?"

"Somewhat. Mostly I'm trying to bother you," she said.

"You're gifted."

"They put me in the 'Gifted and Talented' classes as a kid."

"Me too. Ya ever notice how full those classes were?" he led.

"Mine was bigger than the regular class," she followed.

"I always envied the attention the regular kids got."

She raised her head to one side considering the proposition. "Yeah, it was always as much or as little as I would have wanted."

"Yeah."

"Yeah." She gulped down some coffee and then took a spoonful of soup. "So, how's the heart condition carrying on?"

He rolled his eyes, then cleared his throat and sat up straight, smirking. "You know what, I think I'm comfortable without any insurance for the time being."

"Really?"

"Yeah, the plans usually aren't comprehensive."

"Oh, I see." More soup.

"And, for the price, you can't get a better prescription than—"

"Johnnie Walker Red?" she finished.

"Ha. I would have said Green."

"But you said, 'for the price.'"

"Shit, I guess I did," he laughed between bites.

"You're right, I think. If you're still that shut down, better not to try to meet anyone for a while," she said and extended her arms to crack her knuckles.

"Thanks for not telling me I'm an idiot."

"You don't seem like you want to move on. And if you did, nobody would be into...whatever you're doing right now."

"Sheesh. Yeah, thanks for that."

"Don't mention it," she winked.

He slid his half empty salad bowl to the end of their table and crossed his silverware over it. "You've got the better of me a few times here."

"Wasn't really all that tough."

"I guess not. You know, it's good to kick a man when he's down – shows character."

She'd started laughing before answering. "Maybe I'm just trying to help him build some here."

"God damn."

"Alright, alright," she stifled more laughs, with and at him. "How's the book then? Got a few hundred pages done by now?"

"Is that a wink I see creeping behind your open eyes?" he asked, scanning her face.

"Not at all."

"What I've got is not nearly enough."

"Aw, why's that?"

"I'm still loathing most of what I can come up with. Publisher felt the same. And I need another few dozen pages and a real story that knows where it's going by the end of next month. I think I've got something now though, for a premise."

"Oh, that's great!" She paused as he sneered against the excitement. "Well, it's something, isn't it?"

"It is, I guess," he shrugged. "Hard to tell if it's usable, let alone any good. This one makes or breaks it for me, ya know? If I can manage another unexpectedly solid outing, I'll really have something going. Bigger prints, bigger expectations…"

"Must be incredibly nerve-wracking," she teased with a smile.

He snickered despite himself. "I guess it is. Careful, I'm trying to preserve the veneer that I mightn't take a thought for the 'morrow."

"Sure – I mean, who wouldn't want to give off that too-cool-for-worries attitude? Especially in your position! I mean, you have one chance to make all of your dreams come true." Her grin widened with each syllable that made him shimmy against the vinyl of the booth. "If it doesn't happen for you now, you may as well give up." She sipped from her coffee and looked around the place dramatically. Then she leaned in and half-whispered, "If it isn't a huge hit, you may as well throw away all your belongings and run away to some far-east jungle! How could you ever show your face again? To your friends, your family…"

He closed his eyes and set his hands on the surface of the table on either side of himself, as if to meditate. She finally let up and laughed with him.

"You know what, why don't we pivot here?" he beckoned. "How's your heart condition? You're what, two months or so into the semester? Met anyone interesting yet?"

She gave a long stare out the window with a flat expression. When she turned back, she smiled wryly. "No, I don't think so. I'm not really going out of my way. Too busy with work anyway."

"Ah, yes, the consummated academic – I mean…"

"Ha-ha. Well, there *is* my lit professor; he's young-ish and, occasionally, very dreamy."

He threw his head dramatically down on the table. "Ugh…For the love of…You had the gall to outline, with phenomenally threatening precision how much a cliché I've become and *you*…"

"Oh, come on, I'm just kidding. I'm gonna go pee. Then, can we get out of here? I want to shower before work."

"Whatever you want to do," he said.

"Alright." She stood up and walked to the back of the diner.

"Everything come out okay?" Their overworked server stood over him and began stacking dishes. She smiled earnestly. She was probably forty-five, her ring finger marked by a distinct band of paler flesh than the rest, which he noticed before giving her a brighter smile than he could remember offering anyone in a while.

"Yes, thank you very much. Here, can you take my card before she comes back?"

She smirked. "Of course." The woman traced the path to the restroom and saw Lily was out of earshot. "She's *adorable*, you guys —"

"Oh, we're not, uh…"

"Oh, I'm sorry. I just figured –"

"Ha," he interrupted uncomfortably. "Don't apologize, thank you – we're close, just not, well, involved."

"But you want to be?"

He paused, gave her a look of fury she could tell was put on, then laughed heartily. "You know, I'm trying to fight my way back somewhere else actually. But she's certainly one of a kind."

"Hmm…Oh – here she comes. I'll be back, hun." She winked as she started toward the station behind the bar.

"Ah, so you *will* flirt with anyone, just not with me," Lily lively sprung back into the booth and reached for the purse she'd leaned in its corner.

"You caught me – yes, it's just you. Otherwise, I'm an incessant slut."

"Understandable. I'm too bookish after all."

"Cute." He shook his head.

"Ready?"

"Just about," he turned to search for the server, who was only paces from them.

"Here you are, dear, good to see you," she reached his card back to him, a bill to sign wrapped around it. "You too, hun," she nodded at Lily before rushing away to another table.

"Oh, come on now, that's cheating."

"I won. You can try again next time."

She puffed.

"Shall we?"

"We shall."

He gestured for her to go on ahead. He saw his reflection in the window of the booth and announced to himself, *in this corner, standing vaguely six feet before his slouch, up twenty pounds from his prime, with a standing record of zero romantic wins and one loss by technical knockout, the reigning, undisputed Pathetic Loser Champion of the World...!*

Lady of the Lake

"You know, I strongly suspect that he's not actually much of a drinker – he's just good at putting it on. Likes the drama – oh, sorry, didn't see you there!" Simon teased from the barstool furthest down their row.

He lumbered past his own seat to Simon's and gave a gentle shove on the shoulder. Silently, he retook his perch and aimed a finger to the ceiling as a signal to the bartender that his glass was nearly half full, and he'd soon need another of any variety of "Glen." The bartender, whose Sunday night was kept busy by the three of them and a group of college kids twenty feet down, had already wrapped his wrist around the bottle.

The walk back from the restroom had taken about twelve minutes. Charlie's was a long and narrow bar that didn't put off the bothersome impression of a history far richer and worth remembering than the night one was having. The bricks and exposed rafters revealed a new place trying to look old but not too hard. They'd been there once before at Simon's insistence – maybe five years earlier, fresh out of college themselves.

The framed photographs were of recent and uninspiring events – an employee's niece's high school graduation; a kid who looked nine or ten, probably the son of the titular Charlie, jogging to home plate on a walk-forced run. Floating shelves lined the hall between the back, where the restroom and an office were hidden behind heavy, wooden doors. On each of them was a series of knick-knacks untethered by theme: a moose bobblehead wearing the colors of the local minor league team, a folded Rodney Harrison jersey, pint and shot glasses for purchase with a blue and black *"Charlie's"* printed on them in a different font from that on the awning outside.

Si had Christopher bound in conversation about how Penny had begun encroaching on his half of their walk-in closet, but while he waited for the bartender to top off his "variety Glen," there was a Gobi of flat distance between them. Through the peripheral image of Christopher, whose eyes looked to be held up by a series of invisible marionet wires, he felt a dull tingle of anguish at the quick surrender of Simon and Penny, not long divorced from the wilderness of their once-impressive ranges of public and private predilections, to a domesticity so tame it made the single men present, even Kenny, the bartender's name tag revealed, shudder at their quests for partnership.

"Hey, tramp," he interrupted back to Simon, "Every drop is the real deal."

The others stifled laughs, Kenny included, and Christopher took the opportunity to turn his body back to center between them.

"I think our new friend here should put you on a timer," Christopher joked, half-seriously.

"Damn. I was hoping you'd kill that bottle, so I could make some shelf space," Kenny said.

From down the bar, one of the college guys, whose accent had to have been exaggerated, called out, "Hey bahtendah, it's been a whole ten minutes, I need anothah drink!" His friends laughed with him.

"Right back with you guys," Kenny muttered, rushing away and reaching to the bottom shelf of the column of rum bottles behind him.

Simon cut through the minute of silence that followed, "So, how's the new stuff going?"

He shrugged and exhaled, then took a sip from his fresh glass. "What I've got is solid, so far. There's just not much of it."

"Fair. Hey, at least it's something, right?"

"Yeah, it's something."

Christopher set down his rum and coke – a double Kenny'd poured into a pint glass – loudly and hissed with a cheeky smile, "Yeah, it's something – but it's not much!"

He laughed and took a drink, nodding. Simon's muted laugh got louder with his unspoken permission.

"Not much."

"You know what it'll be about then?" Simon pressed.

"No, not really. Just feelings. Individual scenes. I can feel them blending together; they feel the same. It's getting closer, I have a line on it now. But nothing's really emerged, ya know?"

"Yeah, I get it."

"Yeah, makes sense," Christopher added, in a lightly slurred voice of reassurance.

He suspected that neither of them really got it.

"Well, what's new at work for you two clowns? Still in living large and in-charge?"

"Ha. A little bit too much," Simon piped back. "Ever since this dickhead got the new gig it's been, you know, kind of crazy. Nobody thinks of me as their superior because I'm, well, not. But I've still got to get them to get their shit done."

Christopher chuckled to himself. "Yeah, honestly, I should have turned the job down. Wasn't very thoughtful of me."

Simon chuckled more exaggeratedly. "Yeah. You should have. Look what you've done to me!"

He interjected. "How's music, Si?"

"Ugh. Let's not start that now. So frustrating."

"I got a text from Pen the other day…" Christopher pulled them back.

"Yeah, she's pissed at you," Simon interrupted.

"Yeah, she said you're getting home after midnight half the time lately, and it's all my fault."

"Called you a 'douche-tool' for keeping me away from her so much."

"Yeah, I'd have thought she'd be thanking me profusely for the favor by now," Christopher said.

"You sure she's not pissed about anything else?" he pitched.

"Yeah," Christopher batted, "Like why you haven't proposed yet? She was probably expecting that shit a month ago."

"She was probably expecting it a year ago, really," Simon looked somber behind a laugh.

"When're you going to do it?" he asked.

"Not sure. I'm thinking New Years – but hell, I haven't bought a ring yet. I don't know."

"Well, just keep us appraised."

"Just keep us abreast."

"Why don't you two just marry each other already? Fuck, it's no wonder nobody else will get involved."

Christopher and he punched Simon on each of his shoulders at once. Simon laughed and returned to his near-empty whiskey sour. Kenny had returned and gestured, with his hands, an offer to refill it. Simon held up a finger of pause while he downed the rest, then passed it across the bar.

"Yeah, that's really the least significant reason you're a douche-tool," he piped up, then laughed to himself.

Christopher and Simon looked at each other quietly, then laughed at how bad the joke was.

He exhaled, "Twats," then joined them.

"Excuse me?" A gentle, meek, mild voice sprung up from his right.

204

The three of them turned to face a short, blonde-and-blue-eyed woman whom they recognized as part of the pack of college kids down the bar.

"Sorry, am I in your way?" he joked.

She took him seriously and nodded that he hadn't been. "No, heh."

He sensed that her twinge of nervousness was put on and smirked to himself in irritation. "I'm sorry to bother you," she stuttered on, "I just, um…"

He raised an eyebrow curiously, half expecting an offer for magazine subscriptions.

"…I'm a really big fan of *Searching for Avalon* – um, kind of a *crazy* fan, actually…"

Christopher and Simon were both managing to seethe and gawk in equal measure without letting it on too tastelessly as he smiled and let her carry on.

"And, well, aren't you…?"

He interrupted her, "Shh. No, definitely not." He winked dramatically. If her giggle hadn't, the similar looks on the faces of her friends, lining a high table behind her, would have given her away, too. He hated being fucked with or flirted with unduly, each in the same manic way. The problem was that it took unique dedication to being a geek to feel comfortable approaching the author of an obscure book in a bar, on spec, and make any kind of conversation. If she was being sincere, he had to respect that. He couldn't blaspheme the demands for an ironic, modern gallantry on which he'd constructed much of his repertoire. He'd rather be laughed out of the bar by a nasty prank than risk the cruelty of his impatience. He also felt proud that he'd considered all this while halfway through his fifth drink.

A faint red crept over her cheeks. He straightened his back out. Her friends had turned away from them as if to offer privacy. His friends hadn't. Charlie's wasn't a college bar. He assumed she was something like twenty-two – but she carried herself like a teenager. The whole thing was difficult.

Her eyes flicked anxiously between him and Simon and Christopher to his left. "Well, I just wanted to say thank you. I'm studying TV writing at Emerson," she breathed and continued as if all the words fell out at once, "and-you've-been-a-really-big-inspiration!"

"Oh…Thank you, Miss," he half-whispered, checking every corner of the place in his periphery for traps. "That's very sweet of you." He swiveled his stool an inch towards Christopher, who'd kept laughing under the rim of his raised glass and kicked his leg in place of a 'shut up.' "Please, excuse my friends here. They tend to act as if every fair maiden whose path ours might intercept—"

"'Is the first they've ever come across!'" She laughed. "See? I'm a real fan! Heh…" She'd gone nearly as red as he was, less the liquor.

"I hadn't doubted you. I promise." He'd stayed hushed and tried to chuckle in turn. *Please, don't say anything I have to reject.*

"Thank you! Um…Do you…Is this where you…?"

"No, hun," Christopher leapt in, "He's only visiting us for the weekend. Big-shot here's too good for the frozen north these days!" Simon and the girl laughed.

Simon answered before he could, "Yeah, guy's only here to – what'd he say? 'Clear his head' – by which he means 'drink all weekend and go right back home.'"

"Well, you do such a bang-up job convincing me to visit, don't ya?" he lashed back.

"Anyway," she carried on, hands clutched behind her back, "Thank you – I don't want to disturb you more; my friends sort of dared me to say something, so, thanks."

Simon stopped her. "Why don't you stay for a drink?"

He wished Kenny could have fished Excalibur from the running sink behind the bar, so he could behead Simon before the snickering request reached her.

"Oh, no, I…couldn't impose."

"You're not imposing at all!" Simon insisted. He nudged Christopher's elbow with his own. "In fact, we were just heading out for some air. Why don't you keep our boy company for a bit?"

Acidic rage washed over his eyes, but he tried desperately not to be rude. He smiled at the woman while his eyes followed the two of them, powerwalking to the door, passing the other college kids and Kenny, all badly concealing smiles.

"Heh. Sorry about them again," he pulled a long sip of Glen. "By all means," he pointed an open hand to the stool beside him. She eyed the seat and then him again, weighing her nerves. "What're you drinking? Hey, Ken?" he motioned to the bartender, who'd assumed a position halfway between their parties and locked onto the Celtics' game.

"Oh…um," She plopped onto the barstool quickly, as if to rip off a bandage, and exhaled. "I was having a rum punch." It was the first series of words she'd not shaken through.

"Sounds good," he said as Kenny rinsed a shaker and started counting.

"I'm Gwen, by the way."

"You're kidding."

"Nope," she laughed lightly through. "Was my grandma's name. Just a coincidence."

"Heh. That's some coincidence."

"It is."

Amy had argued the need to use the name for *Avalon's* hero for a year before he agreed: too on the nose, he'd said; too perfect anyway, she'd said. He'd taken another sip before turning back to face her, and when their eyes met, she'd hurried them back away like a scared child. *Fuck*, he thought. After all, he'd have to find a dignified way to end this before it began.

Kenny presented her with a new rum punch, and she raced to it, pulling both limes he'd slid over the rim and squeezing them into it as if having anything to do with her hands was a miracle.

"So, you're studying for TV. What do you want to write?"

"Well, I…In the long run, I want to write a drama about young people living through plagues, kind of dark and hopeless, but with some gallows humor…maybe. I don't know. But for now, after I graduate, I'm just looking to get in any writers' room. Sappy romance or bad comedy if I have to. Sending out pitches when I can."

"Hmm." She grew more articulate and smoother around the edges as she went on. It reminded him of Sara, if only a little, and he smiled at that.

She was angled halfway between him and the bar and raised a hand to push some of her bangs behind her ear. She lit up bluer and redder under the neon behind Kenny, her cheeks betraying a flush energy long absent in himself. And the less weathering of her point of view he could detect, the more he wished he could stand up and leave.

"What?" She kept smiling and looked at the floor.

"Oh, nothing. You know, that's a very sound plan, and as long as you keep your head up and on straight, I think you'll get exactly what you're hoping for. And I look forward to watching a series like that. That's really a great premise."

"Really?"

"You bet it is."

"Oh. Um…Thanks."

"You're welcome."

She took a long drink with both hands wrapped around her glass and set it back down. Then, they were uncomfortable in quiet for a few moments. They amounted to a half-hour for him. He could only rest on a familiar, mechanical question.

"How would you describe your voice?"

"Huh?"

"Your voice. Your characters' voices. What makes them unique?"

She looked around and rested a fist under her chin, leaning on the bar. The more her nerves loosened, the younger she showed. It bothered him some that he'd been left in this moment as if to find some distraction from his romantic woes. It may have been a lifetime ago, but it was barely a few years since he was in her position. He was closed off to women who weren't Sara, sure – but the only shallower perspective than Simon's would probably be to ignore her. So, he stirred, swiveled more completely to her, and listened harder.

"…And maybe a sort-of remorseful wit. Like someone who's living as if they're more mature than they actually are, you know?" she said. He'd missed the beginning as he'd figured out how to be the most respectful he could. But he considered the frame of mind and felt disarmed by it. "I don't know how completely original the sentiment is yet, but it's somewhere to start."

This time, he answered without hesitating or taking a drink. "I don't know how original any of us is, but that's a lot more so than most ideas I've heard lately."

She perked up and gave a faint smirk of thanks. "Maybe." It was the half-tease of someone who'd long figured out she wasn't being flirted back with but wasn't any more ready to leave. She returned to her drink.

He reached for his phone in a moment of silence and found messages from Christopher, who'd seemed the less blotto between himself and Simon before their "fresh air break," which had now gone on twenty minutes:

You're such a lucky piece of shit. What the fuck lmao.

What the fuck man, she's a strong 8 or 9. GTFO.

Are you fucking kidding me? You're still inside?? When are you leaving? We're waiting for you… Couldn't help yourself, huh?

210

Sorry to mess with your moves, boy, Si says he needs to get home, Pen's annoying him on the phone and he can't even answer it correctly lol.

Leaving…text me you're okay, I'll leave the door open…;)

He answered tersely. *Very funny, Fooligan, she's practically a child. I'll get the T. See you soon.*

"Well, Gwen, I have to apologize, but my silly friends are, apparently, not feeling well, and have asked to go. It's been a pleasure talking with you."

"Aw, okay. Thank you. Um…"

"Hmm?" Her friends were waving all sorts of hand gestures at her. She was trying to ignore them and make him ignore them.

"Could I, uh…Give you my number?"

"Oh. I, uh…You know what?" He fumbled. "Here." He threaded a cocktail napkin from its holster atop the bar and scribbled his email address on it. "I don't make a habit of talking with women besides my girlfriend and my mom too much…" She did a wonderful job quieting her scowl behind another drink of her punch. "…But I'd be happy to talk about your writing if you'd ever like to go over an idea or need advice. Is that alright?"

"Heh. Wow. Yeah, sorry…" She sat up. "Yeah, that's great. Thank you." She extended her hand. He shook, stood from his stool, saluted Kenny, who'd left Christopher's tab open, and started out. He smiled at Gwen's friends as he passed them. They chuckled at him. He shot a threatening glare at the hearty, fake-accent guy, who diverted his attention from Gwen.

If you resent the friends whose successes are more temporal, tangible, reliable, and forthright, you're on the road to becoming a total prick or have already arrived. It's true that nothing worthwhile can be culled of envy, but it's especially stupid to levy jealousy at that handful of guys you might know who would stop traffic for you. If you're looking at those guys, knowing that there's an immeasurable, mythological love between you, and still possess the gall necessary to channel your own dissatisfaction into resentment for their victories, pack it in. Jump into the street and tell them not to follow. Better yet, do it when they're far away, so they can't waste their time trying to save you against your wishes.

When their successes include being socially irritating assholes, make sure they succeed at your expense before anyone else's.

Paris

Because the disgust in this kind of egoism is transparent, because it's vile, but in none of the redeeming ways something could be vile, I only sometimes admit to myself that I think of many of the people and days I race past as a series of punishments and rewards in a grand mythology. It alleviates, in some small splinter, the frustrations extracted from revelations that that kind of control is absent from every sliver of life.

If others share this perverse, insular view – which I suspect they do – they aren't direct about it. They fear the social reprisals levied their way upon the reveal that, to them, their friends and family exist only to propel the semi-linear, Campbellian plots of their awfully everyday struggles forward-ish. I don't blame them. To feel unthreatened by the thought of losing a spectrum of social currency is a phenomenon more than a few short meditations away. Though, I do feel at least a little confident that everyone feels this way, and that the reason it's so tersely swept over and seldom noted is that we all share this suspicion about everyone else. It's a guilty business, all of us walking around like the main character with the knowledge that everyone walking past considers us more likely tertiary, if not an extra. What a despicable conclusion we must draw – that there's no story, and we'd be very unlikely its hero if there were. Them's the maths, kids.

He reread the page twice. He moved to crumple it but stayed his hands. After dogearing it, he marked the top, "Worth doing again."

It was half past eleven in the evening when he groaned to stand from the couch, cut out the sounds of *Kind of Blue* with the off button of the CD player, and shuffled to the kitchen to refill his drink. It was near Christmas. He wrestled with a sense of urgency he knew should be stronger. He drew his phone from the right pocket of his shorts and dialed the most recent call.

After some extra rings, Christopher picked up. "It's late."

"What're you, a Quaker?"

"I work at a *real* job."

"Skank."

"What do you want?" Christopher asked, his voice half awake.

He sipped and slunk back into the couch. "Well, I don't know, I was hoping to make jokes about the slow demise of the republic, maybe compare notes on the lesser 'Star Wars' films."

"Gonna need plenty of air-quotes for some of those 'films.'"

"Many, many air-quotes."

"Well, I can for a little bit," Christopher said.

"Thanks."

"Can we really consider the death of the republic a loss?"

"No, no, I meant to celebrate it. It's almost erotic to watch something that's so consistently underwhelmed its expectations finally sigh its last."

Christopher chuckled and stuttered, "Ah, okay. Right. Right."

"Right."

"You know, it would help if you just tried anything new."

He groaned, "I don't want—"

"No, listen, as long as you're keeping me up," Christopher interrupted. "You want to throw yourself down a well, so you don't have to see everyone moving past into new lives, you go right ahead. But you already know where you're going. This is just stupid now. Beneath you. You have to *ascend*. Treat yourself like your own fucking characters."

"I have them do that, so I don't have to."

"Well, you're an idiot. It's not going to work. You think you can get away with this shit because, so far, you have. But

215

you're going to hit that wall – maybe not being able to come up with anything good for this long *is* the wall," Christopher stopped to let him think before continuing. "And if you don't decide to make a change or two – stop thinking about her for a while, stop drinking so much – you're gonna have a hard time climbing out later."

"This isn't about her, come on."

"What *isn't*?" Christopher mocked, "Don't be absurd."

"No, really, come on, man," he pled.

"People don't keep themselves on lockdown just in case their ex comes back."

"Sure they—"

"Not this long. It's been, what, a year? Jesus Christ, man, this is fucked up."

"It's not."

"Okay, let's say you're right. Let's say there's a shot Sara actually gives you that call back, and says she wants to get together and discuss things, right?"

"Yeah," he huffed and planted his glass on the coffee table loudly.

"Okay. Do you think she'll be totally enthralled that in that year you've done fucking nothing to change except drink a fuck-ton? Why would she be moved to give you another shot based on who you are now versus then? Seriously."

He thought a while and Christopher didn't interrupt him. "I guess she wouldn't. And I wouldn't blame her."

"Shut the fuck up with that shit, man. That's what I'm talking about. You've been keeping yourself from making changes because you want things to go back to how they were, and they're not. Even if she comes back."

He leapt to the optimistic version. "If she comes back it has to be different anyway, sure."

"So, why do you think you're keeping yourself from changing, really?"

"Are you suggesting I'm holding myself back because I don't want her to think I've improved?"

"More or less." Christopher occupied a shuttering space between smug knowingness and primal foreboding. He raised his voice. "Lily – Mrs. Suddenly-Best-Friends – what's that really about?"

"It's about friends."

"Psh. Yeah, you're real outgoing, especially lately."

"Christ," he shook his head. "Yeah, I'm not into her. I like having a connection with someone about the work I do, what I read. It doesn't take effort not to be into her. It's really not about that."

"I don't believe you. Because I think you're a liar."

"I'm not lying," he insisted.

"We will see."

"Let me lay it all on the line for you, old boy."

Christopher scoffed. "By all means."

He grinned to himself and muttered quietly, "See, everything like this is just a test."

"Sure."

"No, really. The Fates are testing my honor."

"This chivalry bullshit isn't actually cool or interesting," Christopher said, exhausted.

"No, fuck that, it's not about that. It's about my own honor and glory."

"Alright."

"Listen."

"Okay."

"Are you listening?"

After a grunt, Christopher said, "I'm trying to."

"Good, alright."

"Go on, then."

"Right, yeah." He waited a few dramatic seconds. "I'm not interested in badmouthing anyone. I'm upset, not angry. I'm hurt, not taking aim. It doesn't help me to take out my inadequacies and loneliness on Sara or on Lily or anyone else for that matter."

"Just me," Christopher said.

"Fuck off."

"Psh."

"But yeah. Just you. And sometimes Si."

"And sometimes Si."

He continued, "Sure. It just doesn't do anything for me. I'm miserable, sure, and it doesn't feel like I'm admitting anything by saying that."

"Because everyone knows it, if not by evidence, then by default." Christopher laughed alone at his joke.

"Cool, thank you, sure. No, it's because I think being totally miserable for a while is the right thing to be. I don't think I'm admitting something I should be ashamed of – it's just where I am. I'd like to feel differently. I'm not putting on a front."

"Not that you know anyway."

He shrugged. "Well, I can't – and won't – argue that negative."

"But it's not a negative," Christopher said.

"I'm not arguing it right now."

"Fine."

He twisted and cracked his back, focusing. "Anyway. Are there real mythological Fates and Muses testing my whims and priorities? Probably not, no. But I'm channeling the sentiment into the way I consider myself and my work. I have to, I can't explain it."

Christopher didn't wait to answer. "I can explain it: you're a dick."

"Unrelated to that."

"Oh, okay, fine."

"Thank you. Okay," he said. "So, it's more important for me to decide for my own sake that I'm going to be a good man and that I'm going to do my best with what I have."

"That's all *noble* and *fun* for you and your ego. I'm not following why that means you can't decide to make some changes that make you happier," Christopher repeated.

"That's the point, though. It's a penance. Clearly, I've done something, or multiple somethings, to encourage the Fates' wrath or for my old friend Calliope to forsake the epic scales of my tales."

"Whom?"

"Yeah, yeah." He let go of a laugh despite himself.

With a deep breath to take aim, Christopher shot back, "Look, you know I haven't been the kind of guy to pour vapid bullshit in your ear all this time. I haven't given you the whole 'you've gotta move on, man, there's plenty of fish in the sea,' I haven't even mocked you for neglecting the advantage of the tiny scrap of recognition that I still can't believe you actually have and for not trying to meet women that way."

"Thank you very much."

"You're welcome. And that's because I know that Sara's the be-all and end-all and that won't change for as long as you don't want it to."

"Yeah, that's sort of the point," he said. "Why should the fact that she doesn't want to be with me change how I feel? I'm not bothering her, I'm not intruding, and I'm not acting like an obsessive freak in my own life – I just know I don't want to love anyone else, to share all this strange life with anyone else."

"I get that, I do. But you don't see a problem with what you're doing to yourself, even subconsciously, to keep that up?" Christopher asked.

"Like I said, it's penance. I was never perfect anyway."

"And she was?"

"She's who she means to be. I have to square myself with who I am and who I can be."

After giving him a chance to reconsider the thought, Christopher poked again, "And if you can't pull yourself out of this?"

"Then I wasn't man enough for her anyway – so I may as well find out."

"Fine, so it's not Lily, or anyone or anything else. You don't want fresh air? For yourself – unrelated to Sara. You don't want to find new ways to live? To be more efficient and passionate, to feel alive again?"

"I do, I do," he mumbled. *I only, truly, don't feel I deserve it yet.* "I just have to find my way, and I don't want the way to compromise my hope that someday...yeah."

"Fine."

"Fine."

"Well, you're pitiful and hopeless, but a sufficient Homer character, I guess."

"Thanks," he grumbled.

"Not much of a soldier, though."

"Maybe I'm Paris."

"Jesus. Look, I might be pissed that you're keeping me up to reiterate how much of a pathetic tool you are, but I won't let you call yourself Paris," Christopher attacked in defense. "That's just not right. At the least, you're Menelaus. I mean, at least he had a wife he couldn't keep."

"You're right. Thank you." Slumped back into the couch, he folded his extended drinking arm back towards his mouth and sipped.

"Great. Okay, so I'll talk to you tomorrow," Christopher said abruptly, for the joke of it.

"Alright, thanks."

Memory sparked by something inaudible, Christopher asked, "Are you coming up here for Cody's thing?"

"I don't know. Whatever, honestly."

"Yeah, but I feel obliged to go, which means you should feel obliged to go." Attached to this plea was a series of similar excursions from college to which, at his own insistence,

Christopher attached himself, despite early-morning obligations and late-night work. "Lest we forget that Halloween party on Riva, *Gilderoy*?"

"Not among my most popular costumes despite the weeks I spent on my Branagh impression."

"I've known you nine years, and it wasn't in the top ten."

"Yeah..." he sighed a laugh.

"Yeah."

He calculated the kind of party it'd become and reluctantly gave in. "Alright, I'll probably go."

"Goooooooood," Christopher bellowed, long-winded.

"Ha. Alright. Talk to you later."

"Yeah."

"Thanks."

"Yeah."

Christopher ended the call first. He examined his glass and stood up suddenly. He marched to the sink and emptied the glass, then rinsed it and left it in the dishwasher. In the bathroom, he splashed cold water on his face. He lifted his t-shirt over his head and threw it to the floor, studying his figure. His chest was deflated, and his stomach had grown, despite how little he'd been eating. He scratched at his scalp and felt a stray hair loosen in his palm. He stared at it, not in paralysis, but as if called to action. His five-o'clock shadow had grown scraggly. He turned the knobs of the shower. While the water warmed, he drew a razor from a drawer under the sink and exhaled at himself in anger. Then he blinked a few times. When his eyes stilled, they looked a shade more colorful.

Without thought, he threw his fist into the tiles of the bathroom wall, to the right of the sink. He was overwhelmed with pain and found two of his knuckles open and swelling. He teared and then smiled at his reflection, picking up the razor with his other hand.

Annihilation

"Yeah – no, of course, I understand…No, don't be silly.
Yeah, another time soon. Absolutely…Okay, yeah, go ahead.
I've got some stuff to take care of here too…Alright. Speak to
you later…Yeah, bye." With a flat expression he hung up the
phone and slid it into his pocket.

"And who was that?" Lily purred from the other side of
a textbook collection of classical literature. They were packed
into a two-seat high-top in an extra full Coffee Bean. She hadn't
moved her head or her eyes to ask, which he figured more
likely a sign of her knowingly teasing his desperation than of
her immersion in Edgar Allen Poems, the implied self-pitying
importance of which she didn't like at all.

He faked devious smile. "Agent. He said the publisher
will give me as long as I want – I never have to worry about a
deadline again – I'm getting an extra ten million advance, and
I don't have to make promotional appearances anymore."

224

Only her eyes looked up at him as she lazily laughed along and kicked his nearer foot under the table. "Sounds like a great deal."

"Yeah, not half bad."

Tracing his bandaged hand, he noted the two weeks he had to write thirty more good pages with a quiet laugh.

She scanned his fist on the table and said nothing except, "By the way, are you doing anything this weekend?"

"For once, actually, yeah. Bit of a get-together up north."

"Oh." She returned her gaze to the book.

"Did you want to—"

"I was wondering if you'd want to go to this cool bar I heard about. Some other time."

"Yeah, sorry. Maybe next weekend?" he suggested.

"I'll see about that. I'm having my cousin visit for the holiday."

"Alright." He rubbed his bruised knuckles again.

"You should get back to work anyway. Good discipline and all that – you don't want to get complacent and lazy just before you make it big." She rolled up the sleeves of her oversized blue button-down as she mocked.

He choked out another laugh, stretched his arms, cracked his neck, and crouched back over the notebook in front of him. More of the lunch break rush swarmed into the cafe and they did their best to block out the rummaging and conversation. They'd finished a round of tea and espresso – her reading unassailable, his page highlighted by a single, heavily crossed-out line of prose. But that was before his phone call. Now his hand ached and he tried to savor it.

After, when he leaned over, he dug his pen deep and fast into the paper and the table shook a moment. He apologized when she glared at him and continued more carefully.

I don't want to hear people complaining about their intimacies that don't work out unless they've already been annihilated. You have to be totally annihilated to know whether you really want to be with someone. To know what you really want. You might think, 'Huh, that rather dismisses the point of being with someone,' and you'd be right. But, still, that's how you know. If you haven't been obliterated in your basic thoughts and functions, you can't really know how you'd feel about someone if you were to be – so, you can't know what you feel. There'll always be a part of you, one you don't often hear, whispering in one ear, 'What would you do if it all found a way to get worse? What would you let yourself become?'

Too ugly for you? Put it this way, then: Try to imagine being torched in the soul by moments of dishonesty, neglect, callousness. You've felt them, you've felt the people who delivered them. Can you trace them? Can you trace their motivations and look at them with an all-seeing eye of hindsight and admit where their choices or absences weren't their fault? Where they had no choice, often because of your own?

If you can, maybe you can also predict the next series of realizations: You're at least equally to blame for the unhappiness someone else has caused you; you've drawn it towards you, made yourself a conductor for the malice transferred between footsteps and phone calls taken or unmade. You've made it inevitable that the people you love the most would impose them upon you by magnetizing the forces around you with your own vitriol, summoned from the expectation of cruelty and deception. And, as long as it's your fault, what blame can you parse out? Isn't anger and resentment just a mechanism for letting your own blame go unpunished and your own mistakes go unresolved?

I think it makes more sense to take on a regiment of tithing. Allow the annihilation and do not resent or regret during or after. Struggle to breathe, to wake up and go to bed and carry on, for a while. If you allow yourself distractions, make them the kinds that require sacrifices: Drink and eat enough to create consequence. Don't take new people seriously, regardless of the purpose or interest they might take in your life. If you would find someone attractive, don't. If you would find someone compelling, ignore them when you can. Hold yourself back from the clearest steps forward and doubt your ability to take them.

During moments of clarity, between the annihilation and the tithing, remember everything that led to it. Remember your confusion, the sense of injustice, the rage, the aloneness. And remember how it was all your fucking fault to begin with. You brought it upon yourself – for needing them to make you whole, and for letting them know. On the other bank of that river of memory is one of two realizations. The first, that you're on your way to letting go, moving on, and getting over. The other is that you were always right about them, and you've only continued on loving. Sometimes, I've hinted to people that I've found only more love on the far banks, and they say that I'm crazy and I shouldn't be such a wallowing fool when I've got so much more to look ahead to. Sometimes, they say that not all my dreams can come true. That's the problem for me, I guess – I've never had another dream that couldn't come true somehow. I never thought annihilation meant that the river might stop running and pool up around my ankles, weighty and milky grey, keep me wading in the near bank with a mirage of my dream painted over the shoreline but never getting any closer. A Promethean deadline for a man whose dream had sparked but was set aflame far away.

"Looks like you have something there," Lily said, pulling him from inside the pages.

"Yeah."

"Wow, you even said so without mocking yourself or saying it was shit."

"I guess," he sighed.

"What's wrong?"

"It was a hard one to get through."

"May I?" she reached for the notebook cautiously.

"I don't know."

"Then I won't."

He smiled and almost showed his teeth. "Thanks."

The crowd had sifted out, and only a few other tables remained occupied, also by students and other regulars who worked on unusual schedules or none at all.

Lily closed her book and rested her chin on her hand, looking at him while he sadly stared past her. He'd folded his asymmetrical hands under his elbows and left the notebook alone. She grinned and snatched it.

He exhaled but didn't fuss. The resignation signaled that he'd wanted her to read it but was afraid of the result. *May as well get it over with.*

She scanned through it quickly, then started again from the top, studying the phrases. He was grateful that she was so practiced – maybe she'd only say certain lines were fluffy or indulgent and not ask him questions about…the whole damn thing.

"Hmm," she finally muttered through a long breath, then looked out the window, then to the menu above the coffee bar, then back to him.

"What's the damage? How rough?"

"It's a little much, but it can be smoothed over. This is probably the opposite of the review you wanted, but I'm more interested in the content than the form."

"Fuck, I was afraid you'd say that," he laughed through his exhaling.

"You're decent enough; you know that. I'm not…" she held up his notebook to emphasize her focus, "*here*, but you're also less good than you think. But probably better than other people think, by a little. Whatever, that's not important."

"Sounds pretty significant to me."

"I mean, well, just…Wow."

"What?"

"Someday, I've got to *see* this girl," she locked onto him.

"Ha…Why?" he wondered aloud.

"I mean, one of the last things you described here – that people think you're crazy for learning to love someone *more* after…yeah. That's interesting. I hope you write more about it for this. But she must really be something," Lily said, her eyes meandering.

"You sound like my grandfather, elbowing my ribcage as women pass by in the mall or at the beach."

"My mom always does that to me with guys."

"Ugh." He followed passersby through the window in dark overcoats and remembered how he'd loved the winter once.

Lily laughed hard. "Yeah – no idea how she and my dad got together. He's so Calvinist. I'm lucky she had better sense then."

"Ha. I guess so."

"So, yeah, she must be, like, Helen of Troy or something."

"You might say that," he rolled his eyes.

"Hmm. You're such a horrible platitude. All this anguished whining because you're mad and worried she's become another city's princess."

"Jeez. Well, thanks for phrasing it politically."

"Sure," she threw up her thumb. "You do enough damage to yourself."

"It's just…It's not that simple. I swear, it's not like that," his voice deepened and focused as he went on.

Unapologetic, Lily considered out loud, "It is, but you're used to thinking about everything in these giant, fabled terms, so you fit this into whatever the myths are for it. You're the wounded hero, the beautiful, warrior's future turned to tragedy because you put all your eggs into one queen."

They laughed at the phrase as it came out. "This is strange advice to get from a female friend – and you, of all people," he said.

"It's your own advice, I suspect," she said. "Maybe from the side of your head which is trapped underneath all that overthinking and deluded romantic idealism."

"Youch, woman, no need to flay me, too."

"Heh. I like to. Your skin is sensitive. Ripe for it."

He laughed with a twinge of impatience and stole back his notebook, closing it and putting an elbow over it on the table. "Don't you have homework to do?"

Grinning madly, she answered, "Finished."

"Want another?"

"Yeah."

He stood from the table, and she tried to hand him a five-dollar bill, but he brushed her hand away. In line, he brought his phone to eye level and stared at the Recent Calls log, which read 'Sara' in the space nearest the top. He stared at it a while, thrilled it was there at all, devastated by the cancellation, fumbling towards limbo.

"Yeah," he said to the barista, unfamiliar, probably new, "Can I have two shots of espresso – separate, single shots – a large, unsweet, iced green tea, and a large, iced tea with a shot of simple syrup?"

"Uh...Suuuure," Candy stammered out, grasping at various plastic cups and typing the order into her computer. "Both teas larges?"

"Oh, yes, sorry. Thanks."

"No problem...Just a moment." She ran his card and handed it back.

"I broke up with my only serious boyfriend because he was getting upset that I didn't want to have sex with him."

His eyes glazed back to her across the table. Another hour had passed, this time Lily had put her books away and started writing herself. He hadn't conjured much, mostly staring out the window at the clouds rolling past. "Uh, okay."

"I'm sure it sounds, I don't know, childish or something. To you."

"I'm sure I don't know what you mean."

"Oh, please. Have you ever written anything that wasn't about fucking?" a raised eyebrow evolved into one of her eye rolls.

"Uh…" he dawdled between a blush and a laugh.

"Weren't you the one telling me that everything in the world, ultimately, channels back down into the lowest of our higher ideals – how we can get off?"

"Well, I…maybe."

"Ha. Yeah. So, anyway," she sipped her sweetened tea. "That last little selection of yours made me think of that for some reason. I didn't resent him or regret our relationship really. It had become long distance. We got together when we were seniors in high school. He was the very handsome, over-accomplished member of the drama club who was sure to get into one of the great acting schools. I secretly liked sports and Dungeons and Dragons."

"Growing up without sisters, I guess."

"Yeah, maybe," she answered halfheartedly. "Anyway, when I came here, we agreed to talk all the time and visit as often as we could, but I could tell after the first visit that our little connection was already fading."

"Happens," he offered a forlorn, distant stare of longing for her to empathize with.

She didn't seem to notice. "I guess it does."

"So, why didn't you want to?" he asked.

"Sleep with him?"

"Yeah."

"Well," she started and stopped. *Was that a blush?* "It's not what you think – I don't necessarily want to wait for marriage or anything. I just…I don't know, is it really so unreasonable to want to be more confident about how seriously I take my relationship with someone before it goes there?"

"So, you haven't?"

"Nope."

"Ah. Well, in a way, I'm pretty envious," he muttered, unsure why he'd thought or spoken it.

"What? You? That's a lot to regret, all things considered," she laughed.

"I don't sleep around."

"Oh, I know," she stuttered, "I'm sorry, I didn't mean…" She saw him chuckling at her discomfort. "You know what I mean."

He rubbed his aching knuckles. "Heh. I know."

"Asshole."

"Sorry."

"What makes you envious of that then?" she said, hands over the margins of her notebook.

"Well, I think everyone wants it to be a miraculous, revelatory experience, and no one totally has that, but it's still a nice fantasy. I don't blame my younger self for poking his head in so I can think, 'Hey, wouldn't that be nice to try again?' But it's hard to undo disillusionment."

She shook her head with a grin. "Ah. Understood."

"Well, what was it about this relationship – how long was it?"

"Two years."

"That's a while," he said.

"Sure, most of it was spent far from one another, though."

"Sure. Well, you still got to know him pretty well, I presume, staying together for a long time."

"Sure." Lily nodded and stared into her half-empty plastic teacup.

"And you said your 'only serious relationship,' so you haven't had one in the, what, two or three years since?" Anything to think of someone else's problems, he realized.

"Almost three."

"So, what was it that made you unable to take that step with him?"

"Hmm." She looked past him and up to the rafters while she thought, her mouth scrunched to the side. "I don't think I'd have thought it at the time, but maybe my subconscious knew it wasn't going to work out. And somehow my body told me not to."

"Interesting. Did you ever get close?"

"Sheesh, very prying on this subject, aren't we?" she glared.

"Hey, it's the only thing I write about, remember? I need material."

"Uh-huh." Her glare turned to a teasing smile. "Anyway, yeah, it got close during that last visit. I was home; we were on the couch in my parents' house watching a movie. Everyone else had gone to sleep; we sort of started up."

He shook his head, "Alright, alright."

"What? You can write a million pages of icky details, but I can't talk about it for thirty seconds?" she said.

"Nope."

"Why?"

"Because from what you started with, he sounds like a tool."

"Sure." This eyeroll was fuller. "Yeah, well, anyway, it got to the point where there wasn't much further we could go without…yeah. And then, without warning, I started to get cold and felt a huge distance between him and me, so I moved away and apologized, and we argued."

"He argued with you about that?"

"Yeah."

He folded his arms and rested them on the edge of the table. "That's kind of despicable."

"I thought so too."

"And you broke up with him?"

"We kept talking and seeing each other – in the digital forms available – maybe another month or so. Mostly, it devolved into the same argument about how, 'eventually, we're going to have to…'" It was angrier than he'd yet seen her.

"Ugh."

"Yeah. I tried to say, 'hey, what if I just want asexual companionship forever? What are you going to do about that?'" she laughed.

"And what did he say to that proposition?"

236

"He suddenly got very quiet over the phone and then claimed he had something to 'go take care of' with his roommate. I had it all figured after that, all jokes aside."

"I don't blame you," he said. "What a tool."

"Yeah. Oh well."

"I have to say, having also been pretty asexual for a while, it's got its rewards."

"I think so, I've been enjoying myself. Time to myself. No pressure, and all that."

"Sure."

"Anyway," she sighed after a long minute of silence, "I don't feel resentment or regret about him, or that relationship, nothing. I don't love him anymore – I seldom think about him. But I learned what I had to from that situation. And now, kind of like you said nearer to the beginning, I've become better at being who I want to be, so I'm grateful for that."

"I'm not sure that's exactly how I meant that," he poked back.

"Ha. Well, sometimes, someone sees something different through your words from what you see."

"Believe me, I know." He smiled at her arms, folded on the table to mirror his.

"Do you really love her more now?" she asked.

"Strange to think about, huh?"

"I guess it's not. You had everything you wanted; now all you want is everything back."

"More or less. *Shit, is that it?*

"And you're not afraid that even if you get her back and all those dreams, you could just be annihilated again?"

"The fear did strike me. But I've had a long time to weigh that against how I feel without her, and well, the math wasn't hard."

"Yeah," she trailed off, avoiding his eyes.

"What?"

"Nothing."

"Lil, what?"

She scrunched her lips again before relenting to answer. "It's funny. You're not all here in front of me. It's strange. Part of me feels like, after really getting to know you and being very intimately honest with one another, I still don't know you. I know the shades of you that you allow everyone besides her to see. You're a fragment, a sliver, you know? I know you feel it, see it in yourself. The only whole of you there is, is all hers."

"I'm sorry."

Lily smiled. "There's nothing to be sorry about. Maybe she'll come back, maybe she won't – but you've definitely reached that myth of longing you want for yourself."

"She said *that*?"

"She did."

"Jesus *Christ*." Christopher was driving home from work and the intermittent connection made his speakerphone's clarity and volume adjust without warning. "That's in*sane*," he said with only a little extra gusto, but the phone spat out "SANE" a few decibels stronger. He laughed along to the unwitting exclamation.

"I was totally frozen, no idea what to say."

238

"How did she sound and look when she said it? Like did she—"

He already knew the answer. "No, she didn't look, like, defeated or sad. It wasn't like she was wishing we could be together, blah blah blah."

"Oh."

"She seemed like she was trying to help fix a lost puppy. I felt pretty pathetic actually."

"Well, she's an asshole," Christopher said flatly.

"No, no, really. It was all well-intended. Nothing but concern there. I just realized..."

"What the rest of us have been telling you for months?"

"Uh, yeah."

"Yeah. Dickhead."

He kept up his living room pacing and muttered, "Ha. Yeah. Sorry."

"Well, then. You've finally had your little revelation. You're doomed to love no one else for the rest of your life because you've decided that you're not going to and believed it for so long that it's stained your whole outlook beyond repair."

"Uh, that's not what it means or how I feel," he said.

"Oh, really? Explain then."

"I'm *fortuned* to love no one else for the rest of my life, because I've decided—"

"—Yeah, yeah, okay."

"Ha."

239

"So that's it, then?" Christopher asked, "You're just going to let yourself be like this forever? You can't even work like this."

"Actually, this afternoon I wrote some of my favorite stuff I've written in a long time."

"Really? That's great – but, still, you can't actually live like this. You don't enjoy anything. Look at how you're taking care of yourself."

He thought. "I don't know, I just have to do what I feel I can live with."

"Wait a minute."

"What?"

"Wait a minute, here."

"What."

Christopher took a long moment to respond; he pictured Christopher's familiar, frantic weaving between other commuters as he shouted, "*Fuck you, you fucking bitch!*," and "*Get the fuck – I'm already over here!*" Then he settled. "This is the first time you've told me you really liked anything you've done for, what, a year?"

"Sounds right."

"And this afternoon you were having this little heart-to-heart with Lily?"

"Ugh. Sure. Yeah. Don't give me this."

"Don't be *daft*, you dummy!" Christopher yelled as he did his traffic combat.

"I'm *not*. I've thought about this a thousand times."

"You've lied to yourself about it."

"I want Sara back desperately," he said slow and loud. "I'm not trespassing on her life until she agrees. Maybe she never will. That doesn't mean I have to love anyone else in the meantime. There's plenty more to life."

"That's very *nice* of you," Christopher said with intermittent jolts, angry focus on the wheel. "That's very *brave* and *unique* and *loyal*, all the bullshit you talk about. But it's none of the things you actually *want*."

"Pray tell, what do I want instead?"

"You want, as you put it, the honor and glory of your success, you want a modicum of happiness, and you want to see the way towards the future."

"I don't believe I said that," he countered.

"In so many words."

"Well, what do you think can bring me towards that stuff if I'm not sticking by the principles I've come to define myself by?"

"*Fool!*" Christopher yelled in a parodying, dramatic, half-English accent. "The glory can only come from you actually *working*. A modicum of happiness can only come when you realize you're not happy as you are but could be some other way. And the way to your future is through finding that."

"And you think it's Lily? Someone I'm demonstrably uninterested in?" he said.

"Sure, you're uninterested in her. You've spent a few days a week with her for months after barely seeing anyone else for more months. You've said she's among the most intelligent, tasteful, and attractive people you know – but conveniently qualified those assessments with, 'just not in the ways *I* would be interested in.' This is all nonsense, you sad, sad, little boy. You like her. You like her a *lot*. And you know you do, and you know that you're lying to yourself as well as to me – which is worse."

He laughed, but Christopher went on.

"...And you're lying because of this antiquated, self-fulfilled prophecy of virtue that you think will right all the wrongs in your world if it can come true. And you know that, too. You're a liar. Neither Sara nor Lily seems to like a liar – that's a bad look for you."

With a real twinge of fury, he threw back, "Oh, fuck off."

"You're not arguing."

"There's nothing to argue about." He did some math within a breath. "She is all those things – a really fantastic woman and she'll be happy with someone else. She's become a great friend quickly because she's a good and unjudgmental listener. Our shared interests give us plenty to talk about. I'm not punishing myself, at least, not in this, and I'm not denying ulterior motives or feelings. I'm not mistaken about my grandest feeling. I've never been wrong that Sara is it for me. Someday, those glimmers will align the right way."

Christopher sighed. "Fine, then. Just take better care to survive until then."

"Now *that* is a real question we have to ask."

"Ah-a!" Christopher's laugh went unanswered a long moment.,

The sincerity of his worry exposed, he finally said, "I'm doing okay, old boy."

"I'm not sure you are, now."

"I swear I am." *No use in repeating these circles again.*

"If it's not Lily, it can always be someone. If it's not this idea, it can always be another book. Find ways to make it through for now. That's it."

"I'm doing my best," he was earnest.

"Sure. Just think about what I said before."

"But I'm already trying not to!" he got them both to laugh.

"Ha. Alright. I'm getting near home. I'll talk to you later on."

"Alright. Thanks, *fool*."

"*Knave*." Christopher hung up and there was a lot of quiet.

The Junque Party

Is it possible that the fantastically unattractive posturing of oneself as depressed possesses any merit? Take house parties: they seem designed to accommodate, pretty well, the moments after two or three drinks in which reflections about yourself begin to tilt the evening – in the form of dimly lit extra bedrooms or basement corners into which one can separate himself and really grind his hate: when one isn't past the threshold of sloppiness for which an evening ought to be remembered, but often can't be.

Bars and clubs miss the privacy and noise control of private homes. Let the house become a crowded wilderness of experiments, though, and that liberty isn't for taming. Get past twenty-two, or whenever everyone gets too old for public displays of dirty laundry, and these parties see their truth-or-dare and closet sex and throwing up cheap liquor traded in for serious, guilty admissions and complicated board games and expensive cocktails shaken and stirred by that college friend who tended bar for a few weeks post-grad and likes to tell everyone.

Most of these changes are welcomed – and not just for a guy in his mid-twenties who's recently sworn off truth-or-dare and closet sex (but not cheap liquor if it's all they're serving). It's nice to keep your brain turned on more often and later in the evening. The rest of you might learn something. Anyway, if you're still seeing people after something like twenty-four, you're probably in it with them for the long haul, and you may as well get to know them when they're not blurry.

Yet, the more comfortable people are in their clothes, the more likely laundry will get aired. And by law of average, the occasional glimpses of a once-legendary freak-scene might head its fanciful rear now and again. I like to call these matured exceptions Junque, in homage to an obscure 80s fusion outfit that deserves slightly more recognition at least for its name. The Junque parties are the ones where a few people get more drunk and loose than they meant to, thinking themselves of even greater endurance than they had at twenty, not less. People drink beers on the patio and Jameson-and-gingers in the dining room and whatever's handy in the basement. I prefer a fifth of something dark and sweet in a bottle I can wrap two or three fingers around to leave the others free. Joints are rolled and bragged about, a handful of guys boast about the most loaded they ever got when they see an audience; all sorts of other goods and services are smuggled for the sake of a stoicism no one remembers agreeing to.

"Not every romance is a Greek tragedy. Not every connection you make is going to be so intense. And, by extension, you have to be ready if the one who's best for you might just happen to be less climactic."

"That's a real selling point, huh? 'Yeah, hun, you may not be the pinnacle of brilliance I've been searching for, the feminine variant of my rough otherworldliness, but I'm tired of searching, or she couldn't be here, so you'll have to do.'" He grabbed the chrome flask from Simon's hand and downed a long slurp of the unknown potion within. Penny had claimed she'd mixed dark rum with swigs of cinnamon whiskey and Dr. Pepper. It tasted as if she'd forgotten at least one of them.

Attendance at a Junque party was always by demand rather than invite. With something like ten days left before the new year, he'd taken a series of trains to Massachusetts for the third time in as many months and braced himself for judgment of his sloughing body and frozen mind. But there was no getting out of it. At least he'd get outside for a few days.

The confidants who circled him included the couple; Owen – Cody's and Alyssa's neighbor, recently-adoptive father of a closet of sweater vests, whose prediction of a 'humble soiree' had evolved to its usual policy of 'all the rage' by 7 PM; Kim, a local friend of Owen's made familiar face by the rate of the parties; and the Brothers Swiserton: Sammy, the soft-spoken, sweet, boyish blonde who still looked seventeen, and tall and heavy grizzly-man Tommy, "The Turk" – who nicknamed himself, a nod at the *Godfather* character, after introducing the heavy stuff to the crew's otherwise relatively PG-rated outings of strip-gambling and heavy drinking. The pair were identical, opposite twins, college party legends who wore their ancient, crimson and gold eagle insignias on every sweater and accessory possible. They all snickered at Simon's lighthearted debate.

"That work on you?" he smirked over to Penny.

Penny was already on her way to being thoroughly smashed and laughed much more emphatically than his joke demanded. "Not at all, but lucky for him, I was already into him." She used the button-hem of Simon's blue and red flannel to tug him a foot closer and started obnoxiously kissing his neck and ear.

"Jesus, hey, freaks, get the hell out of here with that," Owen chided with only a little bite to him. "I just washed the floor." He'd spilled half his drink on it ten minutes before.

Penny found the nearest light object – a tissue box, fallen to the floor sometime earlier – and threw it at Owen, flipping him off and sticking out her tongue and then resumed her one-sided making out.

"Hey, give them a break," Cody boomed, coming down the stairs, "Living together only gives them so much time for that."

"Ah, Co," Sammy squeaked, his high voice endearing but still odd after a decade. "You just missed it."

"Si thinks I should forego the whole, 'I've never felt the same way about someone before' sentiment, and, instead, go for, 'I've totally felt this way before; let's see if it works this time," he said, laughing along.

The chatter peppered back and forth, Simon too conservative to indulge Penny's lips on him in public, Sammy and Owen trading drinks and comparing their sweetness, and the Turk gently dabbing his finger in a Ziploc bag on the coffee table between them all, inhaling a bump of coke, offering it to the rest of them to decline in sequence. Cody motioned to follow with his arm and walked into the adjacent office. He closed the door behind them.

"What's up?"

"Everything alright, man?"

"Yeah, what's wrong?" he sensed half a panic.

"You see C upstairs?" Cody said.

"Getting annihilated?"

"Probably, but he's talking to that blonde girl, what's her name?"

Now he sensed half a streak of envy. "Fuck if I know, man."

"Candy? Carly?"

Ha – there's no way he doesn't know. "Carly, I think. Who's she here with?"

"Alone, I thought."

"Oh yeah? Wouldn't have thought. She's cute."

"Oh, really? Why, did you want to talk to her instead?" Cody suggested with a smirk.

"Ha! Hardly. Barely spoke with her, seemed like a nice girl. Think he likes her?"

"Hard to say." Simon laughed under his breath. "This is looking like Junque already."

He took a deep, sharp breath and exhaled it out of the side of his mouth as if from a cigarette, not to blow the scent of rum in Simon's face. "Yep. Looks like a big one. Let's make sure it stays cool."

Cody belted his laugh. "You and me, baby, the soberest of the place."

"Should make people shiver."

"Should but doesn't."

They paused to enjoy one another's company uninterrupted a moment.

"Who does that Carly girl know anyway?" he said.

"I would assume Owen; seems like she's from around here, maybe a neighbor. I don't remember her from school or from any of the other parties."

"All your parties up here have better conversation. Hope Gary has another one soon."

"Yeah, I miss him this weekend, too." Cody took a long slurp from his plastic cup.

"Hey," he gave Cody a sober look as best he could, "What's the story with the wedding? Everything all good?"

"Yeah, man," Cody knew he wasn't convincing but was too drunk to try harder. "We just figured, you know, a couple issues with catering and coordination, probably better to just push it a little. And a spring wedding's probably better for the weather anyway."

"Yeah, man, yeah, for sure. Hey, you let me know what I can do setting up, alright?"

"Thanks, man. Sure." Cody didn't seem like he wanted help from him. "Anyway, let's see if C's gonna make a move and if it works."

"He's still got it, baby, just needed the confidence."

"You say something to him?" he asked.

"Just reminded him that he's big-time cash, and his third or fourth rum and coke did the rest."

"Ha. Nice. Alright. Let's figure it out."

"How're you feeling tonight, man?" Cody asked, patting him on the back.

He forced a grin. "Like seventeen dollars."

"That's pretty alright, I guess."

"Yeah, last weekend I felt like, maybe, eight."

"Alright, we'll take it," Cody said, shaking his hand and molding into a half-hug.

When they emerged from the office, Penny had lost her button-down and was fiddling with her shirt's thin straps over her shoulders. Simon's eyes had begun to glaze over, but his drunkenness was made clearer by the absence of his efforts to over-clothe his girlfriend in a panic. The Turk and Kim were under control still – enough to egg Penny on, anyway.

"Stay safe, you guys, we'll be right back. Pen?" he turned at her.

Penny's eyes widened as she looked up at him.

"Keep your clothes on, will ya? I imagine no one else will ask you to." She was already red. He climbed the stairs with Cody two loud steps at a time.

In the kitchen, Christopher was pouring a rum and coke while leaning over the sink. To his side was Carly, wearing a pair of high-waisted jeans under a baggy 'Nirvana' t-shirt, her hair pulled back with a few strands dangling loose – a look they had all agreed, sometime before, was underrated, somehow. The t-shirt though, he thought, demanded interrogation. If he started listing obscure tracks from *Incesticide*, was that a test she could pass? Perhaps she could – or perhaps she'd prepared the look and the music for the evening.

As he approached them, ready to make jesting compliments to Christopher and help Carly feel welcome, a furiously excitable Jamie Miller intercepted him. Jamie knew how to handle himself. He had a strong upper body, and if liquor or any variations of inhaled herb ever got to him in any volumes, he'd never shown it. He was also more confident talking to women – and men, new friends, potential employers, strangers in the supermarket – than any of them.

"Yo!" Jamie grabbed onto his shoulder. "You've *got* to try this vodka, it's black raspberry-flavored!"

That was the thing about Jamie. You'd never think the social butterfly with the widest, most colorful wings to remember the most intimate, inane details of everyone, like his favorite unpopular fruit flavor.

He stopped in his tracks and took the plastic cup Jamie held out. "Oh, wow – thanks for remembering, man. Awesome." He gulped healthily. "Damn, that's phenomenal."

"Isn't that *sick*? Gotta love it. So, what's happening; what's new, man?"

"Just work, man." He exhaled and peaked around the room and through the hall towards Christopher, who had Carly laughing in fits. "Actually, to be honest, it's going real badly, and I don't know what to do," he laughed at his own directness.

"Ha, I'm sorry, man. That sucks. Do you want to talk about it? Maybe brainstorm?"

Jamie was great.

"Nah, that's okay, J. Let's just enjoy ourselves. That'll help. What's new for you?"

"Ah, nothing special, man. Just got a new contract for work, that's been going well. Just trying to stay healthy and enjoy myself. You been seeing anyone?"

"That's awesome. I'm so glad to hear that. And, uh, no, not really. Not really trying, for now."

"Still hoping about you-know-who?"

"More or less."

"That's good man. As long as you know what you want. Like, take Christopher: he *definitely* knows what he wants," Jamie said.

"Haha – yeah, seems like he does. Have you overheard any of that? How's it going?"

"Looks pretty damn good right now, I've got to say. Sorry I cut you off. I figured you were gonna go mess around – just seems like he's doing fine. I think he's gotta do it on his own."

He smiled at Jamie, then looked at Christopher and back. "You're definitely right about that. Good thinking, man."

"You wanna get another drink, man? Let's find some people to chill with. You seen Si?"

"Ha, yeah – actually, he's sweating over Penny taking her clothes off for some drinking game downstairs." He poured the mixture past his lips again.

"Oh, shit, really? Why don't we just head down there?" Jamie tugged in the direction of the stairs.

"Haha. I'm not really trying to see all that. Turk's looking kind of wild, though. Maybe he's down for some more drinks."

"I'm not drinking with Turk, man. I'm trying to wake up tomorrow."

"Hahaha."

"Haha. Alright, how about them?"

"Who the hell are they?" he wondered.

Jamie had pointed to two brunettes walking through the sliding glass door from the patio. Their faces spelled unfamiliar.

"No idea, let's go introduce ourselves."

"They're just randomly here? Who invited them? Does Cody—"

"Come on, man, just shut up and be a wingman, will ya?" Jamie tugged again. "Let's have a fun time. You're not here to meet anyone, right?"

"Only for you, J." *Fucking hell, J.* He relented and followed through the hall.

"You love me 'cause I make you get out of your head."

Hardly, but that's a nice thought. "Yeah, yeah. Let's get to it."

Steps from the glass door, Jamie commanded the mood to shift. His wide smile and booming laugh carried right through the thumping Top-40, pedestrian shite someone had played too loud. The kitchen to their right was full of sloppy people aiming for refills; in the living room to their left, a dozen or so gathered around the coffee table, some occupied by a card game, others setting up a karaoke machine. Following Jamie through a crowd was magnetic. It felt as if everyone was looking at them in awe, but also as if they had total anonymity in a sea of familiar faces – a disguise that afforded them *total cool*.

"Hi, ladies, I'm Jamie. I didn't recognize you and wanted to make sure you'd been welcomed."

"That's very sweet. Hi, Jamie, I'm Sue, I work with Alyssa," the first of them answered, very warmly. Jamie glowed at her attentiveness right away.

"I'm Sam. I came with her – actually, I'm kind of new to everyone here, I think," the other butted in a little awkwardly.

"Hi Sue, Sam, pleasure to meet you both," Jamie kept on going. "Don't feel new at all. It's a big crowd, but everyone's very friendly. You could start talking to anyone at all and be very at home. Watch."

He and the new girls nearly had to shield their faces in embarrassment as Jamie swung his arms toward the living room.

"Hey, Cal," he called out.

"Yo?" A tall blonde guy poked his head out from group to answer.

"This is Sue and Sam," Jamie pointed at them in succession, "They're friends of Alyssa's. Say 'hey.'"

Cal waved at them and smiled. "Hey!" He returned to the game.

"Ugh, that was excruciating, J," he said.

"Ah, sorry – I forgot. This is our resident sad writer," Jamie laughed along with himself, presenting him.

"Jesus, what a great first impression I always manage to make," he said, shaking their hands. "Shall we get you both something to drink?"

They looked at one another, then nodded. "Thanks," Sue waited for Jamie, then followed to the kitchen.

The kitchen had started to empty, but Christopher and Carly were still laughing back and forth as they drank next to the far counter. Jamie led their procession there.

"Ah, Christopher, Carly – this is Sue and Sam, friends of Alyssa's and now, the rest of us."

Christopher scrunched his face at the interruption but overcame himself and shook their hands with a smile. Carly did the same.

"Now," Jamie went on, "Can I offer a vodka with fruit punch? That's what most everyone's having." He could always call someone's preference from afar – what a guy.

"Careful now, you guys," Christopher chimed in. They looked at him curiously. "J, you're undoubtedly one of my favorite people, and I love ya. But, you know, you're also an irreconcilable slag."

After an uncomfortable silence, the group burst into laughter.

Christopher smiled at his success. "You should be applauded for your dual-citizenship."

The laughs continued.

"What's going on, guys?" they were interrupted by the boisterous, blasted voice of the Turk. "Hi there, I don't believe we've been acquainted," he launched at Sue and Sam.

"That was rather by design, I think," he said back, to snickers from Jamie and Christopher.

"Yo, Turk, they're Alyssa's friends," Jamie proceeded reluctantly. "Sam, Sue, this is Tommy Swiserton. We just call him Turk."

"Hi there," Sue took lead again. "Why do they call you 'Turk?'"

"That's better left to find out later, I think," Carly said. The cackles that followed were led by Christopher and may as well have been applause.

"Yeah, yeah, real funny guys," Tommy said through sniffles and clearing his throat. "Just be careful, ladies. Jamie here is a real easy guy to like. In fact, I think he's one of the least discriminating guys I know."

They all kept laughing, Jamie included, as he poured and passed around more cups.

Hours later he scanned the dark hallway that spanned from the bedrooms to the kitchen, bisecting the top floor of the house. He needed to relieve himself urgently after drinking the balance of half a bottle, spread out over drinks handed to him by various onlookers (and the water needed to carry on). The bathroom door had been closed for twenty minutes, the light inside highlighting its outline. *Whoever's still locked in there is having a much harder time than I am,* he considered. He headed for the stairs to the basement.

The area where Simon, Penny, and the others had been drinking was empty. A few doors outlined the perimeter of the basement – mostly closets, it seemed. One, Cody had told him, was a second bathroom. They were all closed, but he saw and heard no traces of life.

He opened the first door he saw – a small closet stuffed with winter coats. The next, right beside it, was filled with moving boxes. Across the room was another. He sped to it, ready to restrain his urine with his hand if this door, too, was a bust. It wasn't, in a manner.

"Oh, fuck yes – oh, fuck! Shit!"

His hand was frozen a moment on the handle as he took in Jamie, Sue's legs wrapped around his waist, and their sudden horror. Jamie's was considerably less than Sue's. She'd reached for a towel to cover her bare chest on instinct; Jamie'd turned his head to the mirror that faced the door and smiled a laugh. He pulled the door closed. "My humblest apologies – carry on," he managed on autopilot. He took large steps back to the stairs and held his crotch with one hand, trying to hide the motion under his baggy, button-down shirt.

At the top of the stairs Christopher was waiting, looking both concerned and pleased with himself at once.

"What's up?"

"She seems really into me," Christopher stammered.

"That's great – can we please talk about this in a moment? I need the bathroom, and both are occupied, so I'm panicking."

"Just go use a tree."

His nose shot to the air. "And you like to call me disgusting."

"Emergency, man. Battle conditions. Go ahead."

"Ugh. Yeah. You're right. Fuck." He pivoted towards the sliding glass door but heard another door crack open and turned back. An unoccupied restroom. "Ah, thank fucking God."

He didn't see whoever emerged. It didn't matter. He jogged down the hallway – more of a fast waddle – and slammed the bathroom door shut.

After relieving himself, he washed his hands, then his face, then threw water over his hair to guide it back. He studied himself. It was the first effort he'd made to look decent in months. It felt better than he figured he looked. He laughed meekly at the humbly pathetic version of himself, then returned to the hall.

Christopher was gone. *Probably carrying on someplace with Carly – perhaps in a closet downstairs.* Changing tactic for some fresh air, he started towards the back door. It was blocked by a very high and giggly Turk.

"Woah, woah, where ya goin', man?" the hulking gargoyle yelped.

"Just wanted some air, man, what's up?"

"Ah, nah, nah, you're not going out there right now, man," Tommy said loudly, his eyes searching the rest of the living room for no one in particular.

"Who are you, the fucking River Guardian?"

The Turk's focus went to the ceiling as he considered the title. "You might say so," he turned back, quiet and serious.

"Why don't you come get some fresh air with me, man?" he gave up.

"You know what man," Tommy looked around again, skeptically, "You might be right. We should go outside, right now."

"Yeah, alright."

He led the Turk outside. Another dozen people surrounded a fire pit, passing around joints and bottles. One of them was playing an interesting series of scales on a nylon-stringed guitar. *I should find her later and note that that section in Lydian was very cool*, he made the mental note already predicting he'd forget it. They stepped down from the patio onto the lawn. Turk produced a pack of cigarettes and offered one. He nodded them away.

"So, what's happening man?" Tommy puffed and started to settle his frantic moves and mouth. "I hear you're still not over this girl."

He rolled his eyes the way Lily did. "Not exactly."

"Well, why not man? It's been a long time."

"Heh. You know, I'm still in love with her. Not really trying to get over her."

"Oh yeah?" Tommy didn't pace or tilt his body back and forth as he stood, he was totally still. His expression changed like normal, but his eyes never looked elsewhere.

"Yep."

"That's a little fucked up, man."

"Why?" He was more fascinated with Tommy's ramblings than he was upset. They weren't close enough for this type of shit, but, at this point, whatever.

"Do you think she's waiting around for you?" Tommy asked.

"That's not really—"

"Cause she's not, man. Hot girl like that, if she left you, she's looking for someone else or already got him."

"Alright, look, Tommy, shut the fuck up."

Turk took another hit of his cigarette and put up his other hand to signal a white flag. "Nah, nah, man, I'm sorry – I'm not trying to be a dick. I'm just smacked right now. Just, listen."

"I don't think I want to, sorry."

"I'm serious man, alright? I'm sorry. Just, please, give me a sec."

He huffed and stayed still, waiting.

"I'm sorry, I just mean...Don't you think you should at least be having a good time right now? Trying to, you know, not be so fucked up and, I don't know, negative, all the time?"

"*You're* gonna tell me not to get fucked up all the time, Tommy?"

"Yeah, and if *I'm* saying, you know you're fucked up."

He shook his head. "Ha. Fine. Fair. So, what're you proposing? You offering me some of your shit again?"

"No, no, you're too pussy. I know." Another long drag.

He scoffed.

"I'm just saying, why don't you try to hook up with someone? I mean, look at everything going on right now? Actually, a pretty stacked party, isn't it? Jamie's getting action as usual, looks like Christopher's got something going, all the couples already...People are getting wasted, hooking up, enjoying themselves. And you're just walking around getting shitfaced, nothing to show for it."

"The one I want to be with is not here right now," he said plainly.

"Yeah, man, she's not. But, for all you know – and I'm sorry, alright? – she's out there at a similar party, hooking up with some guy just because he's not you." Anticipating a punch, Tommy put his hands up. When nothing came, he continued, "And that's really fucked, and I'm sorry, man. But you can't feel shitty about everything all the time. You've gotta let yourself feel good sometimes, or you're gonna get real fucked up."

Fuck off and die, Turk. "Thanks for looking out, Tommy. I'm not looking for that right now. But I appreciate what you're trying to do."

"I'm serious, man." Turk threw the second half of his cigarette to the ground and put it out under his boot, then pulled another from its carton and lit it. He put it in his mouth as he cautioned on. "You're all romantic and that's great man. But, sometimes, you've gotta be able to just fuck. Screw around and enjoy yourself. Don't make everything so important. You're still getting some eyes, you know. Most of these guys are wishing they'd get that, and they fucking hate you. Maybe you should stop mocking us with your bullshit for one night."

He gave pause but only a moment's. "I'm not gonna argue with you, Tommy. You're right for everyone in the world, almost. But I know what I want. And hey, maybe you're right. Maybe she's out there really living it up without me, and yeah, that makes me feel…not great." He paused again. "But, if I dig down in me, I know it doesn't change how I feel or the fact that I want to end up with her. So, ya know, I'll just figure things out."

Tommy shrugged. "I hope it works for ya, man."

"Thanks. You too."

"You want a hit?" Tommy extended the new cigarette.

He waved it off. "I don't smoke, thanks."

"How 'bout a bump? Or something else? Got some other tasty things."

"I'm good, man. Be fucking careful, will you? Christ."

Tommy laughed. "I'm just looking for a good time, you know that."

262

"Yeah. I'll keep it in mind."

He wheeled back up the patio and into the house. On the way he thought he saw Christopher and Carly jaw-locked on the other side of the yard. He smiled and kept on.

He reentered the living room and studied it. The music had been replaced by something club-suited and bass-heavy. The lights had been dimmed or turned off, the card game foregone, and rambling karaoke had taken over, inaudible under Cody's impressive speakers. A pair of unfamiliar faces connected on the couch. Others sized each other up through their drinks.

Sam was doing her best impression of welcome and occupied but couldn't stop looking around uncomfortably. Some in the living room were trying to include her, but it wouldn't take. She stood at attention when Sue and Jamie rejoined the party, and he pitied the discomfort with which she was about to be inflicted.

Instead, though, Cody and Alyssa, flushed and vaguely sweating, also reappeared, and Christopher and Carly helped them all form a circle. Something needed to be done so that the sex half of them had just finished with could go neglected in conversation.

"Jesus," he acted as if he'd lost his breath in a climactic scene. "Got held up by Turk by the door. He looked like he needed some fresh air before he exploded."

"Haha. Sounds about right," Cody said.

"He tried to stop me getting through the door. Started asking me all kinds of personal questions. I don't think he realizes how over-qualified he is to be dispensing riddles from under a bridge."

The circle laughed and kept drinking.

"The problem with Fleetwood Mac is they've ruined the prospect of collaborating with a lover for everyone else. Imagine that shit happening post-Mac. Imagine you're crazy about someone, you join a band together, it goes great, and then you break up. It's ugly as shit. You're each writing brilliant shit about the other. But then, instead of buying the thing, everyone just says, 'Who the fuck do you think you are, Fleetwood Mac?' You think another *Rumours* has any marketability post-*Rumours*?" he said.

"Yeah, no, nobody's buying that story again. Just sounds like they're copying them," Christopher said.

"Yep. Shit won't happen again."

Christopher, Simon, and he sat on floor around Cody's coffee table, each of them doubling up on liquor and water. Penny dozed on the couch, her clothes still on, an arm wrapped around Simon's, who had his back leaned on the couch. All bark.

"Do you think the guys who prefer virgins are really interested in the whole 'being the first' thing, or is it more about not having to face the insecurity of being lesser than someone's used to?" Christopher pitched.

"Yes."

Simon laughed at the readiness of his reply.

"I don't think I know anything especially worth voicing about women, but if there were an exception to that, I'd say women find someone without a sense of definitive self fantastically unattractive."

"Why's that?" Simon asked.

"I'm not sure."

"Is it because they're looking for a guy who's already secure?" Christopher offered.

"I don't know, maybe. There's more than biology there though, for sure."

"What more is there, really? I mean, I get it, the 'soul' and 'individual experiences' and all that bullshit," Christopher had a sly smile on.

"Well, yeah, it's probably in the range between those things," he said.

"Fuck it, then."

"Yeah."

Penny stirred and they stayed quiet to let her sleep. She woke up anyway, sat up, and nudged Simon, pleading for water. He rose from the floor.

"Alright," Simon announced after a few minutes. "Time for bed. You need a hand, babe?"

"Yes." Penny raised an arm over her head, expecting him to take her, her eyes still shut.

"Alright, come on."

The couple drunkenly meandered from the living room through the kitchen and to Cody's office. They shut the door, and he and Christopher were relieved not to hear anything more.

He leaned towards Christopher. "How'd it go with Carly?"

"Pretty well. I don't know what'll happen. It's a long distance to start anything serious."

"So, nothing went down earlier?"

"What do you take me for?"

"Jamie, maybe."

"Haha. Not quite. Made out. Got her number; we'll go from there."

"Alright, then. Good work."

"Thanks. Night."

"Night."

Christopher assumed Penny's old spot on the couch and passed out quickly. When everything was quiet and he was alone, he walked to the sink, poured the remnants of his drink down it, and sat on a barstool. He dug into the cabinets and found an empty glass, filled it with water, furiously gulped it down, and repeated this a few times.

"Couldn't sleep?" Alyssa asked, hushed as she milled into the kitchen.

"No, not exactly."

"Want more blankets or anything?"

"No, no, it's not that. Thanks, though," he smiled graciously for her.

She was always the only one more stubborn. "What's bothering you?"

"I could ask you the same thing."

"But I asked first."

"I'm just too unhappy to sleep easy right now," he said.

"Just tonight, or in general?"

Maybe she's just wondering if it was a good enough party, he thought. "In general," he offered, barely projecting his voice.

"I'm sorry. Do you want to talk about it?"

"I think I've consumed all of you enough with that."

She approached him slowly and folded her arms. "Ha. Maybe you have. So what? It's important to you, it's important to us."

"Thanks. It's alright though. It'll just keep bothering me until it doesn't anymore."

"I guess so." Her eyes twinkled uncharacteristically. Probably from the pity.

"What's got you up, and down?" he redirected.

She shuttered and stayed quiet a moment. "I don't know. I haven't been happy much recently, either."

"Something with Co—"

"No, no. He's great, we're fine."

"Good." He stretched and reached for a cup, playing Russian roulette with the vodka he knew was hidden among waters but that he could no longer smell distinctly.

Alyssa was quiet.

Finally, he followed, "Are you unhappy about the postponement?"

"Ugh. It's fine. I don't care. It's just…me."

"Yeah."

"I'm allowed to be upset sometimes, aren't I?" she said. "Are things so perfect that I shouldn't be able to be disappointed with myself? Or thinking about what I wanted, what I thought I'd have, when I was younger?"

"You're always allowed to want that and to be upset about it." He sighed and stretched his back out, sitting up straight. "I'm glad you don't decide you're happy just because you guys are working."

She said, a little bitter, "Well, I'd hope we're working."

"Hey, you never know."

"Shut the fuck up! Ha. I guess. But, yeah, you have to be who you want yourself to be. And, hey, Sara's not turning around and waltzing back through your door until you're happy with yourself."

"Yeah. I've been thinking a lot about that. Wish I'd put that together before she left."

"Seems so simple after," she projected all the wisdom of decent filmmaking.

"Yeah."

"You always know it, but you never think they'll leave over it."

"Yeah." He lowered his head.

"I don't want to think about it anymore, though."

"Sure, me neither."

"Penny's not thrilled either," she said.

"I figured as much. I don't think it'll be long, though." He winked.

"Did he say something?" she barely kept hushed.

"More or less. Keep it to yourself."

"I'll try."

"Uh-huh." Another Lily eyeroll.

"I will!"

"If you say so."

"Ha. Dick. Alright. Leave the glass in the dishwasher, please."

He looked around the kitchen, littered with unclean glasses, spilled and toppled plastic cups, left-out aluminum tins of junk food, open bottles and bags of unknowable powders and grains. "Of course. Wouldn't want to make a mess."

She laughed under her breath and flipped him off as she retreated down the hall.

Eve

"Is this some kind of joke?"

"It wasn't good?" He took a drink and then set his glass down on the coffee table.

"Good? This shit's worse than the first fifty!"

"Jesus, are you serious?"

Amy breathed on the other side of the line. "So, instead of good prose and no direction, you took the most played, generic direction you could think of, chucked a hundred sloppy pages at me, and forgot about the prose?"

"Uh…" he flipped through his copy of the pages he'd sent her two days before. "Well, I just felt that it was most important to get a sense of the tangible stuff down first—"

"Yeah, but when I told you tangible, I wasn't thinking this lazy nonsense. Look at this, on page sixty, you have them sneaking into a closet at a party – what is this shit?"

"Well, you know, it's…"

"I don't know anything about these characters except that they're unrelatable, and I don't like them. Fuck, what is this? I don't see or hear *you* anywhere here. Did you ask someone to write this for you? What the hell – it's like someone wrote sloppy fanfiction of your stuff."

"Fuck, Amy, dig a little harder, why don't ya?"

"I'm not fucking around, here! You have a few weeks and, as far as I'm concerned, this is all gone. You can't give me this."

"Shit."

"What the hell is happening?"

"I don't know. I'm sorry. I can't connect the things I'm thinking about to a more concrete structure and it's killing me."

"No shit."

It seemed it was Amy's turn to fear she'd made a bad bet – this time, on him. She'd been kind with criticism before, asking for small changes or suggesting minor sequences to embolden secondary characters. Her cold, flatlined tactics had been abandoned before the call. She sounded like he'd been left alone with the house for the weekend and got caught having a party after staining the floor and smashing a vase. She was gutturally wounded. He couldn't easily explain that he was too drunk to be restored by her disappointment.

"I don't know what else to tell you now, but I'm on a schedule here. I need the whole draft by February eleventh, and I can't make an exception. It can't fall further behind."

"I understand. I'll figure it out and I'll send it." He curled into the couch and stretched his arms.

"Yeah. You do that. Because if it's not figured out, characters, plot, and theme, I can't take it. It won't go to print."

271

As he counted, his attention jangling loosely, forty-two days sounded like a comfortable eternity.

"No problem, Amy. It'll be done."

"Yeah, okay." She was resigned, exhausted. She hung up.

He stood from the couch and saw the time on the microwave clock. *Of much greater urgency, I have to meet Christopher at the train station in half an hour.* To the pile of sweaters on his desk chair, out the door, down the stairs and out he went, invigorated.

Christopher was halfway through buttoning a dark blue shirt as he hung an arm from the bathroom doorway and leaned into the hall. "Ay, this alright?"

He looked up from the kitchen counter across the apartment. "Yeah, looks good."

"Good. Very good. Alright."

He took a sip from the dark-tinted glass on the counter and winced at the ice nudging against his teeth. He swallowed hard.

"She really said she'll drop the book?" Christopher said.

"Yep."

"That's crazy, isn't it? Didn't you do well enough last time that they wouldn't want to?"

"I guess that's how bad I've gotten here. Better not to take any risk on something that doesn't have much ceiling anyway."

"Wow. Yeah, I guess."

"Yeah."

"So, what're you going to do?" Christopher asked, eyes wide.

"I guess I have to write it."

"Well, yeah, but you've been working so hard *not* doing that for a while."

"Thanks – yeah." He chuckled halfheartedly.

"So?"

"Maybe the pressure will make me do it." *I really believe that it will!*

"Let us hope."

"Let's."

Christopher retreated into the bathroom.

"Do you have any backup places in mind, in case the first one is, you know, kind of garbage?" he called through the mirror.

"Yeah, but I doubt we'll need that. Place is supposed to be pretty solid."

"Well, yeah. But 'On the Level' makes it sound like some swanky rooftop place."

"Nah, fuck that. We don't want that touristy bullshit. This place makes great cocktails, some scotch-based stuff that even *I* might actually like. And the atmosphere is smooth. Music's not too loud, people respect your space. And anyone worth meeting will be hiding in there."

"I'll take your word for it."

He muttered with a shrug, "I've never been there."

"What?" Christopher laughed, expecting a take-back or some other joke.

"Never been. Heard it's right up my alley."

"Ha. Every time anyone recommends you anything – a TV show, a vacation spot – you smile at them and then say, 'no chance in hell' under your breath."

"Yeah, I hate it when people tell me what I like."

"So, why are we going to this place?" Christopher's suspicion rose mostly in jest.

"Well, Lily's the one who told me about it, and she's, I don't know, sort of immune to that problem."

"Is that right?" Christopher smirked.

"More or less."

"Right."

"What?" he asked, a dare.

"I don't know, just seems a little Freudian to me, *knave*."

"Ugh. Jesus. For the last time – there's no *there* there. She's been pretty spot on with other recommendations."

"Like what?"

"Like a cocktail at another place the other day. That show *Grey Matter*."

"Didn't you say that trailer looked like – what'd you say? – 'fucking unforgivable, melodramatic garbage'?"

He defended, "I did, but she made me try it and it was alright."

"Jesus Christ." Christopher shook his head.

"I don't know what I can say to argue this more. It's not like that. It's like hanging out with you, just without, you know, that next level of honesty and things we've shared. It's cool to have a female friend I'm this close to. Different perspective."

"It's a different perspective, alright." Christopher shook his head laughing, finished rolling up his second sleeve, and poured a similar dark drink into a similar glass of ice. He sipped it. "How do you drink this stuff when you have options?"

"Heh. Not sure." He drew his glass from the counter and drank deeply.

"Well, we'd better get a move on. Nearly ten now. If it sucks, we'll have time to try somewhere else early."

"Sure." He killed the last of his drink and fiddled with his own sleeves, then retrieved his keys from the coffee table.

"Let's assume you're telling the truth," Christopher said between sips.

"Which you should."

"Right. So, let's assume that. How do you know she's not lying about being into you?"

"We've talked about it," he said, pitch elevated, "And I believe her."

"Uh-huh."

"What?" he asked genuinely.

"I don't know – don't you think you're being a little air-headed, even potentially cruel here?"

"God. No. Why?" He led Christopher out the front door, waited until he passed, and closed and locked it behind them. They proceeded down the hall and the stairs.

"It's like this…So, you've both gone out of the way to say you're not interested romantically, sexually…"

"Yeah."

"Yeah, so, why did you feel the need to do that unless there was some obvious tension already?" Christopher said.

"Well, she was the one to say it first. I just agreed, 'cause I was relieved I wouldn't have to rudely make the comment myself later. I had already mentioned Sara to her and my whole situation, so I think it was all pretty clear. Just a matter of respect." He breathed the fresh air in deeply.

It was already a deep dark outside, the street half-alive on a Thursday night with the resuscitation of neon and streetlights. They proceeded down his street and past the Coffee Bean.

"How far is it, by the way?"

"Something like five blocks down and two over," he said.

"Oh, that's close."

"That's why I chose it."

Christopher gave a sly frown. "Sure."

"Heh."

"Alright, so, she did it first."

"Yeah."

"Don't you think that's a little, I don't know – defensive?" Christopher asked.

"How do you figure that?"

"You don't think it's weird? This girl is only a couple years younger than us, trying to do exactly what you do. You're still young-ish—"

He cut in, "Still younger than you, that is."

"By a few months, prick."

"Oh, yes, only five." He huffed jokingly as they stepped over a divot in the sidewalk.

"Well, whatever, you're still young, and much as I hate to say it, still attractive."

"God, yeah, right."

Christopher pushed his shoulder, so he had to narrowly dodge a sign post they passed. "Oh, get over yourself and the self-pity bullshit."

"Never!"

"Ha. Yeah, well, I'm not saying it again. But you get the point. You don't think she was, maybe, hoping something might happen? And then, suddenly, said she didn't want it to because she realized you were going to reject her – which I still doubt, by the way – and, well, didn't want to deal with that?"

"You've managed to frame the real situation in reverse actually," he said.

"Ha. Why?" They stopped to wait for a red light.

"I don't think anyone's really gonna be into a guy who's already past his prime, not as fit or put together as he could be, and generally hates everything about himself. Not the most attractive combination."

Christopher nodded against him. "Maybe to some random person. But to someone who values what you care about, you've got a lot going on."

"Sweet of you. I don't imagine anyone really does. Maybe the occasional hit to every dozen or so misses."

"I just think," Christopher stopped as people passed them closely. "I don't know, I think you're too eager to brush off something that could really be good."

"There's no brushing off. I know what I like." He stopped walking. "Here it is."

"What?" Christopher looked at the signs and design of the building they'd stopped in front of. "This is a furniture gallery."

"Ha – yeah, it's inside. We sit on the designer sofas." He knocked twice, hard, on the second of two doors that faced the street. While the first was glass and led, clearly, to an array of kitchen tables and living room sets, the second was made of forest green-painted wood and had no markings on it. The latches sprung to life and the door creaked open a few inches.

A high-pitched squeal beckoned as he tried to walk through. "Ah-ah-ah…One moment, fellas. Why don't you come back and bring me a stack of cocktail napkins…" The figure fished his hand through the crack between the door and its frame and measured between thumb and forefinger. "About that high?"

Christopher looked slightly bewildered and thoroughly pissed off.

"Uh, sorry?" he asked back. He scrunched his lips to one side as he waited uncomfortably.

The door opened further, and they got a better look at its guard. He was maybe five-foot-four, one-forty-five, early fifties, had a shaved head, and squinted at them so hard they could see all the muscles in his head contracting. His smile was pleasant, though. "Just fucking with ya! Hurry on in, it's cold, ya schmucks!"

They stepped in and the door slammed quick and loud behind them. The bar was narrow and long on their right, extending to the back of the place. A row of black, leather booths took up the whole left side opposite it, and high tables bisected them. The lights were dim yellows and oranges, the walls all brick. There were no televisions or knick-knacks. Guests at the bar clung to a series of peculiar looking cocktails, and those at the tables each gathered around eager, private conversation. They smiled at one another, a confirmation that, despite Christopher's reticence, it was a cool spot. They saw only two tables unoccupied and headed to claim the nearest.

Steps from the table, a woman two booths down could be overheard as she raised her voice, "Well, that's because Uncle Gerry is a fucking *lunatic*..." Their eyes moved to her direction on instinct, and he saw her shoulders tense and her head lower, though her back was to him, in an effort to hide after drawing attention.

Across from her was a black-haired woman who looked twenty-five and equally embarrassed by the outburst though her mechanism for remaining clandestine was taking a sip of her sported mojito and staring down into its glass.

He and Christopher knelt to their booth when he realized it. "Ah, fuckin' hell, I don't believe it."

"What?" Christopher said, still scanning the place for people and tone as he settled into the half-circle.

"Just a second." He leaned away from their seats and gave a disbelieving smile in the direction of the loud women two tables down, then stepped towards them.

"What's up?" Christopher called, following him with his eyes.

The black-haired woman saw him coming and he looked directly at her by mistake. He smiled to make up for it.

"Umm..." she muttered as he neared.

"What?" the other said, then followed the first's eyes to him.

"Oh, well, fuckin' hell," Lily said in his direction. She smiled back.

"That's what I said."

"I bet it is," she said. "Wow. When you asked if I knew anywhere cool…"

"Yeah, sorry, I should have warned you it was sort of urgent," he laughed.

"No, it's okay – um, sorry," she turned to her drinking partner, "Mia," she directed them to each other.

"Is this—"

"Yeah," Lily interrupted quickly, "The new bane of my study schedule."

"Shh," he whispered to them, standing over their table and between the two. "If anyone finds out I'm here, I'm toast. I'm not allowed out of the house until February."

"And he likes to think he's subtle when he talks about his deadlines to remind people that he's famous among twelve people," Lily mocked.

"I guess I do," he said, "One of many bad habits I'm not trying hard enough to break."

"Definitely true," she said.

"And, I'm sorry, Mia?" he said to the other woman.

She extended her hand for a shake. "Yes, hi, I'm Mia."

He shook her hand firmly. "A friend? Classmate? Life-partner?"

She laughed at him. "Cousin."

"From Providence," Lily filled in.

"Ah, yes, Lily mentioned you'd be visiting."

"Just for the weekend," Mia continued. "Nice to meet you."

"Don't be too sure," Christopher said from over his shoulder.

The three at the table turned and snickered.

"Ah, I was about to come get you," he said. "Lily, Mia, this is my dear old boy, Christopher – he's in from Boston."

"For the same reason as you," Christopher smiled at Mia as he finished the thought.

"Ah, Christopher," Lily turned more fully to him, "I've heard so much about you."

"If I know *him*, none of it was good."

"Some of it was alright," she accused. All four laughed.

"That's more generous than usual," Christopher said, side-eying him.

He had already prepared. "I was in a giving mood."

"Would you like to join us?" Mia offered.

He and Lily exchanged a precarious look as the men sat down on either end of the booth. He'd have sensed his friend's interest in Mia even if he'd known him ten years fewer. A smile slipped, and he was grateful its source wasn't clear.

"What're you both having?" he asked.

"A mojito, extra mint," Mia said, stirring as she brought it to her mouth. She left a light pink lipstick stain on the edge of the glass. Her makeup was more exaggerated than Lily's, who wore her usual tame foundation and eyeshadow. At most, only one of them had come barhopping on a Thursday eager to meet somebody.

"And I'm having a scotch, neat," Lily answered, her chin up and a smug, praise-seeking grin stretched over her face.

"That sounds like what I'm getting," he said back. "Christopher? My treat."

"Ugh. The last time you treated me to a drink I nearly spit it back up; it was so disgusting."

"Apologies," he said over the girls' laughs, "I'm not making it this time."

"A Captain-and-Coke, if you'd please."

"Done-and-done," he said. "Be right back."

He stood from the table and took long strides to the bar, already loosened by the buzz from the apartment. Standing at the bar in wait, he looked back to the table, where the rest of them were sharing a joke that, from the tilt of their heads, was made by Christopher, at his expense.

"What can I getcha?" The bartender was something like his age, tired from overwork. He stood at attention looking eager to prepare something and move on.

"Hey, thanks – can I get a scotch, neat, and a Captain-and-Coke?"

"What kind of scotch?"

"Well is fine."

"Word." The bartender fiddled quickly while he waited. He pulled his phone from his pocket to pass the time without rudely staring. He'd gotten messages from Christopher moments before, presumably before he'd followed to the table.

She's hot. Mia, I mean. Well, they're both hot, and you're a fucking idiot, but you know what I mean. What should I do?

He laughed to himself and shook his head.

Talk like a person…She's just a girl; she won't bite.

"Scotch, neat," the bartender spoke up. He raised his head back to the bar. "And a Captain-and-Coke." He laid both down.

"Thank you," he reached for his wallet.

"Do you want to open a tab?"

"No, that's alright; you've got it busy enough," he said, replacing the glasses with two twenties. "I'll be back, though." The bartender nodded his thanks and moved on.

He returned to the table and set Christopher's drink down.

"Ah, thank you."

"My pleasure."

"Christopher here was just enlightening us about, what was it called, the 'Junque party,' you both attended recently?" Lily said with a smirk.

"Oh, Jesus – now, why would you do a thing like that?" he said to Christopher, who was already laughing.

"Well, I thought it was important for more people to know the truth about you. You know, what a total freak you are."

"Ha! Sweet of you."

Mia turned to Christopher. "And where were *you*, again, during this belligerent game of Flip Cup?"

"Yes, Christopher," he said excitedly, "I personally don't recall seeing you while I was making a fool of myself on the patio. Where was it you'd run off to?"

Christopher scowled at him, then contorted his face to something jollier to answer. "Oh, I was just exploring the neighborhood – took a walk with Simon and Penny, some friends of ours."

"Ah, yes, I suppose they were conspicuously absent as well." He laughed as he thought of Simon and Penny, his own teammates for the game in question, and then whichever room of the basement Christopher had been exploring with Carly. Good thing they'd not spoken much since, he supposed.

"So, what is it that makes you such a prolific drinker?" Mia asked him.

"Ah," he swept his palm over his face and left it under his chin, "Mostly legend. I enjoy a casual drink… and allowing people to make folklore of me in whatever respects they'd like."

"Ah, I see," Lily said. "So, you wouldn't be nearly done with that one already?" She pointed at his glass with her eyes.

"Uh…"

"And," she kept on, "You wouldn't be interested in replacing both of these?" She clanked her own empty glass onto the table against his.

"Heh. I guess I would." He stood. "If you'll all excuse me – and, ladies, please disregard everything he says."

"No chance." Lily shooed him away with her wrist, then leaned back across the table to Mia and Christopher, excluding him.

He laughed and returned to the bar.

"Ready for another?" the bartender appeared.

"A pair of neat scotches, please."

"Sure."

He turned back to the table and saw Christopher and Mia leaned over their drinks and laughing, and no sign of Lily. "Blue Train" hovered over his head, and he spent a minute lost in it, feeling welcome.

"Two scotches, neat," the bartender placed them down and took the empty glasses he'd brought in their place.

"Thanks again." He laid down cash again and grabbed the rocks glasses.

"Hey." He felt a hand on his shoulder and knew it was Lily before she spoke. He turned.

"Hey, what's up?"

"Let's step out for a minute?" she directed.

"Uh, alright, I'll just set these down."

"Don't bother," she said, taking hers from him. She brought it to her mouth and slowly drank the whole of the chilled liquor in one go. He smiled at the challenge as she set it back down on the bar. "Alright, then." He copied her and followed her out the front door.

"You know, we've never talked about our backgrounds," he said. They sat on the curb half a block from the bar's wood door.

"Who fucking cares?" Lily said.

He smiled and didn't answer, and they sat in silence for a few minutes, enjoying the calculation of how drunk they'd gotten in half an hour.

"So, did you end up seeing your ex?" she piped up, a little slurred.

"No, she cancelled."

285

"Ouch. Sorry." It wasn't her most apologetic tone.

"More like postponed, I guess."

"When's that gonna happen, then?"

He answered, "I don't know, a few weeks, maybe."

"Well, I hope it all works out," she said.

"Thanks. Yeah."

Quiet again.

"What's it like to be with someone for a long time?" she asked. Like, for real, I mean."

"Heh. I guess I should try telling someone before I forget," he said.

"I just, I don't know, I'm trying to figure out what I'm looking for. You're always so messed up about it, but then you say it's all beautiful. So, which is it? Why should I bother?"

"That's a good question," he laughed loudly, and it echoed to the apartments above them.

He thought for a while, and she looked around at the street.

"I guess, if you've found someone you really care about, more than a passing or physical feeling, as their passions, worries, dreams start to attach to your life, you get wrapped up in how they are. If you really buy in, your happiness is sort of dependent on theirs. And that feeling keeps growing. Eventually, you can't imagine yourself without them. It's empowering and comforting like you might imagine, but it's also, I don't know – reassuring? To know you've got someone on your side."

A sweet smile morphed into an uncertain, clenched frown as he spoke. "That's a lot," she said. "That actually sounds horrible. That's like, possessive. A little crazy."

"Well, I don't mean it that way – although I may have been too obsessive, I admit."

She laughed quietly.

"I just mean," he continued, "Maybe, when the feelings keep growing instead of getting stagnant or tired, it's easy to let that keep building. You don't need to get reliant on them, but they do grow from the trappings of your life – the paintings on the walls, the candles and incense, the gifts, and knick-knacks on furniture tops – to the pillars, the foundation. By the time you realize you're defined as much by the relationship as anything else in your life, it's too late to change it or to want to change it."

"Hmm. Yeah, that's a lot."

"Ha, I know. It's too much, sometimes."

"You put pressure on each other," she decided.

"Well, I definitely put pressure on her."

"How'd you fuck up?"

"I thought it was just, you know, a nice thing to constantly tell her how much I cared and be very vocal. Talk about it a lot. I thought I was reminding her that she always had support."

"But she took that the wrong way?" Dumbfounded by such a criticism, Lily revealed what he could only recognize as a disdain for Sara. Perhaps she'd been a subject of their discussions long enough.

But he had to answer. "Who wants to have to either re-commit to that depth of partnership constantly or lie about it every day? Especially if they're a very independent person. Maybe it made her doubt I was telling the truth, I don't know."

"I can see that."

"Yeah. So, love isn't the problem when you're in a good situation to start with. Communication, sure, but that's everyone's problem. Wanting the same things – that's complicated because what people want changes. But you can talk that out if it's working."

She sighed. "Right."

"And if it's not working, neglecting to talk it out will only make it more complicated before it ends, and it was going to anyway."

"Sure."

"Sorry," he said. "I know this is all just rambling nonsense, it's just all I can come up with."

She was considerably drunk and stood up, shakily, stretching her arms. "Ha. That's alright. I asked."

"Well, have you thought about what you're looking for?"

"Sure. I just doubt it's totally out there. If it is, I'll probably be too wrapped up in my work to notice."

"Yeah, I get it."

She folded her elbows over her head. "I don't know, I like tall, skinny, clean-cut guys, more straight-edged than I am. More into the real world. Family guys, maybe. Like to travel, respect my space and my passion for my work – willing to leave me alone when I need it."

He continued for her, "You're looking for the security of knowing where he'll be, what he's up to, what he wants."

"Yeah. But more, I want something that makes me feel grounded. I don't want to be in the sky all the time, overly romantic. I don't care about idealistic bullshit. I'd like to be direct about what we want and make concrete plans. Otherwise, I'll just get lost in my head and go nuts." She moved her hands spherically around her head in a show of confusion.

"Well, I'm sure you're not alone in that. But, hey, you've got a lot to offer, so he'll happen along eventually. Just do your best to keep true to what you want." He stood as well, stretching his arms over his head, too, and tugging on his shoulders.

"Well, yeah."

"Just don't waste your time with shit you can already see being only halfway what you want. You'll buy in on purpose, try to make it work because you don't want it not to, and it'll be more awful when it doesn't," he said.

"That doesn't sound like what happened to you."

"It's not. And I like to think of it in the present."

"Fine, sure."

"It's not what happened to me," he said, "Just to everyone else I know."

"Oh." She gave him a fake giggle. "That's grim."

"Sure is. Oh, and try not to meet anyone in one of your lit classes."

"Ha. Why lit?" she asked.

They returned to the doorway.

"If you're gonna settle for someone less grounded than you want in the end, they shouldn't be nearly as sure of themselves as you are."

"Ugh, don't be ridiculous." She smacked his shoulder with the back of her hand.

"Ha. I'm just saying you're not exactly easy to argue with, and half of building something up, only for it to collapse under the effort, is surviving semi-regular arguments, couched in polite disagreement, about mundane things turned radically consuming."

"Like what?" she waved to the bouncer, and he opened the door.

"Like the content of, let's say, Jane Austen being five-hundred times more valuable and interesting than the form, which is unreadable if you're not sold on the former."

They paced slowly towards the table to prolong their analysis of its featured pair.

He glanced around the room humming a melody and she raised a curious eyebrow. Upon noticing it he started singing the melody boisterously, "So, turn up the light and burn my wings, watch them ignite and pull my strings," some extra swing to each of his steps.

She shook her head embarrassed as half the bar tilted their heads. "You're totally absurd, and no thinking woman will ever love you if you tell them things like that," she said, beaming anyway. "Oh, this looks great." She eyed Mia and Christopher, sipping cocktails inches from one another on their side of the booth.

"As if this wasn't the reason you insisted upon our excursion," he whipped back.

They smirked as they crouched back into the booth.

"Hey there, guys," Lily teased.

"Hi," Mia answered fast, red. "I actually need another drink." She emptied her last and then motioned for Christopher to let her out of the booth.

"I was about to say the same," he said, rising again. He looked back at Lily, and she waved him off.

"I'm definitely good for tonight."

"Me too. I'll wait at least," Christopher pointed at the mostly full glass in front of him.

"We'll be right back then," he said, following Mia to the bar.

He contemplated the dangers of leaving a drunk Christopher and Lily together without him, each of them armed with the means to embarrass him immeasurably.

"Sorry we haven't had a chance to talk much," Mia burst his daydreaming worry, then turned to the bartender. "Can I get a shot of tequila, please? Silver."

"Uh-oh, going hard now, huh?" he said.

"Just having fun," she said with a smile.

"And don't worry about the talking – I'm happy to see you and Christopher hitting it off." He took his turn at the bar, "Another, please. Thank you, again."

They faced the table. Lily and Christopher were locked in a conversation of similar proportion, and turned themselves to face the bar, all four of them snickering.

"Yeah, he's very sweet. It's funny – I hadn't even expected to meet *you* over this weekend, let alone someone for me."

"Sorry?"

"Oh," Mia sighed, then reddened again, slightly. "Well, when Lily invited me to visit for the New Year, we were talking. Just catching up, you know. We haven't seen each other since last Christmas. Our dads weren't that close."

"Sure, I follow."

The bartender set down their drinks, and he paid before she could. They took the glasses, she nodded in thanks and took her shot, and he sipped.

Shaking her head and gnawing at her lime, Mia continued, "So, she mentioned that she'd made friends with this guy, told me about you, said you have all these things in common...And she just seemed, I don't know, excited. So, I asked if she was into him – you – you know, and she said that she wasn't because he wasn't."

He took a long drink and swallowed hard, looking from Mia to Lily and Christopher and back. "Oh, I see."

"Sorry, I thought you'd both talked about it."

"We did," he said. "I just, uh, didn't realize that that was the exact..."

"Oh, oh *no*. I'm sorry!" Mia giggled through her apology, giving him the distinctly repulsive feeling of being suggested to. "I didn't mean to say it that way. Just forget it, will you?" She laughed through her teeth again. "I mean, meeting you, I, like, *understand*... Ugh, well, never mind – please don't say anything!"

He looked to the table again. Lily was eyeing Mia angrily as if she'd understood everything. Christopher was trying to keep her attention but looked bittered by her shifting attention. He felt horrendous.

"Yeah, alright. Hey, tell them I'll be right back, will you?" He nodded to direct her back to the table, then set his half-empty glass on the bar and left in search of the bathroom.

Around a set of dark hallways, he found it. To his relief, it was uniquely clean. He pulled back the door of its lone stall and knelt to throw up. Maybe ten percent of the bile had built up from liquor, the rest from what a fucking *idiot* he was. He stood and flushed, his stomach empty. He left the stall and found the sink, washing his mouth and spitting, then washing and drying his face. Panic set in at the realization that he'd have to entertain while projecting this kind of disgust. He exhaled in anger at the thought that a line would go unwritten and probably unremembered by the next morning since he hadn't a way of recording it: *I do, sometimes, wish that I could throw up on command. Regrettably, for now at least, I make do with public transit.*

He began the journey back to their table. By some miracle, he found Christopher, Lily, and Mia hovering over the table, bags in hands and coats bundling.

"What'd I miss?" he said quietly as he approached.

"I'm not feeling well actually," Lily said, "Just want to get home and sleep. Sorry to kill the mood."

Mia stepped in, "Yeah, you should be!"

The others laughed awkwardly.

"Don't worry about it, just hydrate and get sleep," Christopher said. "We'll have to do this again."

"We will," Mia said, sloppily winking at Christopher, who smiled back subtly, trying to preserve a note of propriety that had long vanished.

"Alright," he said, ready to press the advantage for an escape. "Do you want me to call you a ride?"

"No, that's alright, we're close enough," Lily said, smiling smally.

That's a big lie, sheesh. "Alright. Just be careful."

"Thanks."

The four neared the door and Christopher held it for the rest.

They stepped out to the street, the girls turning left, the guys right. All of them looked back to wave after a few steps except Lily.

"You said *what*?"

"I told her I could see why you talk so fondly of her," Christopher cackled.

"Jesus Christ, you fucking idiot."

They stood over his kitchen counter across from each other, guzzling water in the hope they could match the evening's new sobriety.

"Why the fuck—"

"I'm not interested in her," he nearly screamed. "I'm trying to get Sara back, you fuckwit."

"You talk about her a *lot*," Christopher drunkenly laughed.

"She's a good friend. I talk about you a lot, too."

"Uh-huh."

"Jesus Christ. Fuck."

"What's really wrong here?" Christopher asked.

"Ugh. When we were at the bar, Mia let it slip that Lily's, well—"

"Ah, I see – she's into you after all."

"I don't know. That's what it sounded like. She might have been doing the same thing you're doing – being a dumb skank and projecting it onto everyone else," he said.

"Hey, hey, stop that!" Christopher put on a fake scowl, then kept laughing.

"I was just trying to nip this in the bud—"

Christopher hadn't stopped laughing.

"I'm sorry, I didn't mean...I thought I was helping out. You have to figure your shit out. She seemed really great. Thought it would be a good thing."

"Yeah, no, I know. I'm sorry for yelling. Jesus."

"And what's worse," Christopher was already smirking as he began, "She's obviously pissed because she knows that you know that she knows that you know."

"Haha. Yeah, shit. That's the real fuckin' tops."

"Yeah."

"Yeah."

They'd settled into the couch and were onto their third round of waters. Christopher, of course, never believed in those but was indulging the effort in good sport.

"Let's just order something."

"The fuck do you want?" he asked.

"Not a pizza."

"Good."

"Chinese."

"Alright."

Christopher sprang up. "Let's order the fucking Chinese."

"We need to get five or six different things."

"For enough variety to make the order worthwhile."

"And then we'll have it for lunch tomorrow," he continued.

"Sure."

"Alright, what do you want?"

"Mongolian Beef," Christopher answered before he'd finished asking.

"Yep." He wrote it onto one of the legal pads on the coffee table, which had something like three or four sheets left untorn and un-crumpled in the corner wastepaper basket. "What else?"

"Some kind of fried rice."

He insisted with a glare, "Just veggies."

"Sure," Christopher glared back.

"What about a General Tso's."

At once, "Gotta get the General Tso's."

"You've gotta."

"Okay. Lo mein?"

"Yeah, plain."

"Okay, plain," Christopher nodded.

He chugged his water, swallowed, and let out a deep breath. "Crab Rangoon."

"No shit. Two of them. What're we, in a prison camp?"

"Jesus."

"Yeah."

"Alright, seems like we need one more." They referred to 'Ocean's Eleven' often.

"Alright, one more."

"I like the tofu dishes."

Christopher got serious. "Shut the fuck up with your bullshit tofu."

"What do you want, then?"

"Wait, where are you getting it from?"

"Why?"

"Is it that fusion place?" Christopher pressed.

"Yeah."

"So, they have that sushi you said you liked."

He perked up. "Yeah. Oh, that's a good idea."

"Yeah, throw on a spicy tuna roll for me."

"Alright, I'll get that and mine," he said.

"Alright, there we go."

"Yep."

"Alright, let me know what I owe you."

"You're calling," he said.

Christopher threw his head to its side. "Fuck that. I hate calling."

"I hate it more."

"So, we'll flip for it." From his pocket, Christopher produced a quarter. "Heads you call, tails I don't call."

"Get the hell out of here," he laughed, "I've got tails. You flip."

Christopher reached for the coin, clenched it and shook it between his fingers for luck. He flipped, and it landed on tails. "Ugh. Fuck you, you bitch."

He laughed to himself, ripped their list from the legal pad, and passed it over the couch. Then he picked up a pen and started writing as Christopher dialed the number from memory.

"Yeah, hi, can I place an order for delivery?" Christopher began. "Yeah, can I get a Mongolian Beef; a General Tso's chicken; two orders of Crab Rangoon; a plain lo mein – yeah, *plain*, no veggies, nothing – okay, thanks; one vegetable fried rice – yeah, vegetables in that one, yes, I *know*, thanks; and one spicy tuna roll and one sweet potato roll. Yeah. That's it. Okay, sure. Thanks. Cash. Okay, thank you."

"What's the damage?"

"Fifty-five."

"Alright, I'll get it when they get here. It's my turn," he said.

"Nah, that's alright. I'll put in the twenty-seven-fifty."

"No, really, it's my turn—"

"Alright!" Christopher jumped.

"Ha. Very good."

"Gotta stand by tradition!"

"We do."

He stared at his blank page for a few minutes while Christopher fiddled with his phone. Nothing happened.

"So," he said, giving up, "Looked pretty happening there with Mia, huh?"

"Yeah, she's really something. Providence is what, an hour away? No problem."

"Sure, worth it if it works."

After a lull, Christopher said, "Maybe I'll convince her to come to Boston."

"That's a little fast."

"Yeah, who cares?"

"Yeah, sure," he shrugged, eyes on page.

"Well, I definitely liked her. Great sense of humor. Super easy to talk to. Very pretty."

"That's a solid, politically-ordered list."

"You bet it is."

He looked down again as Christopher flipped on the TV and sneered at the absence of cable.

"Don't you get tired of watching the same eight movies over and over?" Christopher asked rhetorically, scanning the shelf of familiar DVDs.

"Don't you get tired of being a fucking *skud*?" he barked.

They broke into fits of laughter.

"A 'skud?' Like, a SKUD missile?"

"I don't know, sure."

"Alright, that'll be a thing," Christopher determined.

"That's a thing."

"I'll just put on fucking 'Last Crusade.'"

"You say that like it's a problem," he said, sliding to the back of the couch with a sigh.

"Hey, I'm doing it, aren't I?"

The Paramount iconography spread over the Utah desert, and he scratched over the yellow paper.

Oblivion

Everything between everyone has always
got to be romantic even when they aren't
trying. And when it isn't, it sucks. That's why
it all sucks.

Sunlight on the Garden

A layer of panic had seeped into his flesh and found all sorts of terrible ways out. Through his hair, it shriveled and fell out, and also through a constant wave of sweat that more water – from the shower or by the glass – could not stave off. The deadline was two weeks away, and he had fuck-all to show for six months of work. A few dozen pages of small ramblings he'd labeled "vaguely interesting" in his head were stacked on the kitchen counter behind him. He barely had characters. He desperately wanted not to write more about his love life. Even if he could avoid being utterly banal, it offered myriad other ways to hurt him if he dared carry it over a couple hundred pages.

From the outline of the sun through his blinds, he guessed it was after four in the afternoon. He'd been staring at a yellow page for half an hour, and strangely, it hadn't generated the bits of revelation and genius needed to save his neck on its own. The Coffee Bean called, but he didn't want to see strangers or have them see his body. He settled for a drink, which he filled liberally into a glass he rinsed, rather than setting on the dishwasher. Shuffling his feet across the floor with only a little purpose, he found the stereo tucked between stacks of CDs and DVDs on the second shelf from the top of the bookcase nearest the window. From among them, he plucked a Snarky Puppy record and slid it into the stereo. He returned to the couch and laughed to himself. *Fuck, most guys like me – and there are plenty of them – have had all the same experiences; I may as well not exist.*

Then the phone rang, and he picked it from his pocket on instinct, forgetting how he'd intended to spend the day working and not to allow disturbances. The caller I.D. only read "Lily." He hadn't settled on a sardonic nickname for her, and they hadn't had time to choose a referential one.

"Hey," he said shortly, quietly.

"Hey, what, you're just getting up?" she said, half amused and half critical.

"No, no, ha. Just been struggling through pages for a few hours."

"Maybe you should take a break," she said.

"Yeah, maybe. I don't know, I really wanted to be productive today. Not much time left."

"Yeah, I know. Well, uh…" She stuttered and was quiet. She didn't sound much like usual.

Unsettled, he asked outright, "What's the matter?"

"Well, I uh, I don't know. I want to talk to you about something, but I'm sorry, it's not…Well, it's not a good time. But, I guess, I just have to."

"What're you talking about? Is everything okay?"